COMPACT Research

Terrorist Attacks

by Lauri S. Friedman

Current Issues

ReferencePoint Press

San Diego, CA

ReferencePoint Press™

For more information, contact
ReferencePoint Press, Inc.
PO Box 27779
San Diego, CA 92198
www. ReferencePointPress.com

Picture credits:
AP/Wide World Photos, 9, 11
Steve Zmina, 36–38, 57–60, 76–79, 97–101

Series design:
Tamia Dowlatabadi

LIBRARY OF CONGRESS CATALOGING-IN-PUBLICATION DATA

Friedman, Lauri S.
Terrorist attacks / by Lauri S. Friedman.
p. cm. — (Compact research series)
Includes bibliographical references and index.
ISBN-13: 978-1-60152-022-7 (library binding)
ISBN-10: 1-60152-022-0 (library binding)
1. Terrorism. I. Title.
HV6431.F745 2007
363.325—dc22

2007009907

Contents

Foreword

"Where is the knowledge we have lost in information?"

—"The Rock," T.S. Eliot.

As modern civilization continues to evolve, its ability to create, store, distribute, and access information expands exponentially. The explosion of information from all media continues to increase at a phenomenal rate. By 2020 some experts predict the worldwide information base will double every 73 days. While access to diverse sources of information and perspectives is paramount to any democratic society, information alone cannot help people gain knowledge and understanding. Information must be organized and presented clearly and succinctly in order to be understood. The challenge in the digital age becomes not the creation of information, but how best to sort, organize, enhance, and present information.

ReferencePoint Press developed the Compact Research series with this challenge of the information age in mind. More than any other subject area today, researching current events can yield vast, diverse, and unqualified information that can be intimidating and overwhelming for even the most advanced and motivated researcher. The Compact Research series offers a compact, relevant, intelligent, and conveniently organized collection of information covering a variety of current and controversial topics ranging from illegal immigration to marijuana.

The series focuses on three types of information: objective single-author narratives, opinion-based primary source quotations, and facts and statistics. The clearly written objective narratives provide context and reliable background information. Primary source quotes are carefully selected and cited, exposing the reader to differing points of view. And facts and statistics sections aid the reader in evaluating perspectives. Presenting these key types of information creates a richer, more balanced learning experience.

For better understanding and convenience, the series enhances information by organizing it into narrower topics and adding design features that make it easy for a reader to identify desired content. For example, in *Compact Research: Illegal Immigration*, a chapter covering the economic impact of illegal immigration has an objective narrative explaining the various ways the economy is impacted, a balanced section of numerous primary source quotes on the topic, followed by facts and full-color illustrations to encourage evaluation of contrasting perspectives.

The ancient Roman philosopher Lucius Annaeus Seneca wrote, "It is quality rather than quantity that matters." More than just a collection of content, the Compact Research series is simply committed to creating, finding, organizing, and presenting the most relevant and appropriate amount of information on a current topic in a user-friendly style that invites, intrigues, and fosters understanding.

Terrorist Attacks at a Glance

Prevalence

In 2005 there were 11,111 terrorist attacks worldwide.

Definition

Section 2656f(d) of Title 22 of the United States Code defines terrorism as "premeditated, politically motivated violence perpetrated against noncombatant targets by subnational groups or clandestine agents."

Largest Terrorist Group

Osama bin Laden's al Qaeda operates more terrorist cells than any other terrorist group in the world.

American Death Rate

Americans are killed in about 0.4 percent of terrorist attacks worldwide.

Terrorist Profile

There is no one profile of a terrorist. Terrorists have been husbands, wives, fathers, mothers, sons, and daughters. They range in age from teenager to elderly. They can be wealthy or poor; religious or nonreligious; sane or insane; socially isolated or fully integrated into community activities.

Where Terrorists Come From

Terrorism has been practiced by citizens of Algeria, Colombia, Egypt, Germany, Greece, India, Ireland, Israel, Italy, Japan, Lebanon, Nigeria,

Pakistan, Peru, the Philippines, Saudi Arabia, Spain, Turkey, the United States, the United Kingdom, Venezuela, and Yemen.

Iraq

In 2005, 30 percent of all terrorist attacks and 55 percent of all deaths from terrorist attacks occurred in Iraq.

Suicide Terrorism

The average suicide attack is 12 times deadlier than other forms of terrorist attacks.

Terrorist Attacks and Democracies

The United States, France, India, Israel, Russia, Sri Lanka, and Turkey have been the targets of almost every suicide attack of the past two decades—and they were all democracies at the time of the attack.

Overview

"The provisions extend FBI power for warrantless records searches without judicial scrutiny . . . but is this so horrible? Remember, we are at war. If someone starts reading cookbooks on how to build a dirty bomb, isn't this something the authorities should look into?"

—Paul Rosenzweig, attorney and George Mason University law professor.

"America was founded by men who understood that the threat of domestic tyranny is as great as any threat from abroad. If we want to be worthy of their legacy, we must resist the rush toward ever-increasing state control of our society. Otherwise, our own government will become a greater threat to our freedoms than any foreign terrorist."

—Ron Paul, Republican Congressman from Texas.

Since the September 11, 2001, terrorist attacks, Americans live every day in the world of terrorism. From what threats the United States currently faces, to what motivates terrorists, to what policies and programs can best prevent terrorism, terrorism and its related issues have become the number one topic of concern for the United States. It is likely that terrorism-related topics will continue to take center stage in political, economic, humanitarian, national security, development, energy, and foreign policy discussions. In studying terrorism and ter-

The September 11 attacks on the World Trade Center suddenly made terrorism and national security the top concern of Americans.

rorist attacks, it is important to understand why the United States and its Western allies are vulnerable to terrorism and why terrorism poses unique challenges for open, democratic societies.

Fighting Terrorism in a Democracy: Unique Challenges

Democracies are uniquely vulnerable to terrorism because they are, by nature, open and free societies. People who live in democracies enjoy traveling without restrictions from one point to another; living without constant surveillance; and being granted a large degree of privacy and liberty. But terrorists, too, are able to take advantage of the absence of surveillance, restrictions, and rules, making it infinitely easier for them to move freely, plot in secrecy, and attack the open, unguarded systems available to the public. Terrorism expert Robert A. Pape of the University of Chicago has documented democratic nations' unique vulnerability to terrorism. He has observed that "the United States, France, India, Israel, Russia, Sri Lanka, and Turkey have been the targets of almost every suicide attack of the past two decades, and each country has been a democracy at the time of the incidents."[1]

"At more than 9 million square miles, the U.S. is 450 times larger than the state of Israel, which has been able to implement checkpoints, walls, and other terrorism-reducing tools because of its small size."

A "Target Rich" Nation

The United States is particularly vulnerable to a terrorist attack because it is an enormous country with infrastructure too vast to realistically be able to protect every inch of it. At more than 9 million square miles, the United States is 450 times larger than the state of Israel, which has been able to implement checkpoints, walls, and other terrorism-reducing tools because of its small size.

In addition, America shares 1,933 miles of border with Mexico, 5,525 miles with Canada, and has more than 95,000 miles of shorelines and navigable rivers. According to the Office of Management and Budget, each year more than 500 million people, 130 million motor vehicles, 2.5 million railcars, and 5.7 million cargo containers cross American borders. Six hundred million air passengers travel annually at more than 400 airports, and 61 million passengers arrive on more than 500,000 international flights. Add to this tens of thousands of malls, stadiums, theaters, landmarks, museums, and thousands of miles of rail and pipeline, and it is no wonder that law professor Abraham D. Sofaer has described the United States to the 9/11 Commission as "target-rich," arguing that "our enemies have broad access to us."[2]

How Much Will the Public Tolerate?

Steps have been taken to secure as much of the United States as possible without changing its citizens' quality of life. The largest security impositions have been placed in the nation's airports, and since 9/11 passengers have shown a high degree of tolerance for long lines and invasive security checks that require shoe removal, body pat downs, and belongings searches. Many Americans have welcomed extended security measures simply because they feel the measures could be worth it. "No one wants to live in a police state," writes author Chris Short. "However, . . . the majority of people do not mind being searched if it means they will live another day. . . . The threat of being blown up is a greater risk than the far-fetched idea of a police state."[3]

As of 2007, in most other public spaces security changes had yet to be imposed beyond a few extra police officers, additional security cameras, or a relatively unobtrusive bag search. More extensive security measures had not been exercised for fear of inconveniencing travelers and, particularly, shoppers. Mall security experts Steve Filyo and Leo West write: "Dramatically increased military or police presence at America's

Sports stadiums, like Boston's Fenway Park, are considered high risk targets because so many people gather in one place to watch an event.

shopping centers would present a chilling atmosphere as well as possibly raise certain legal issues."[4]

It remains to be seen whether Americans will ever tolerate the tight, time-consuming day-to-day security that Israelis, for example, are forced to live with. Some security measures have met with skepticism from the public, such as a proposed national identification card that would provide the government with comprehensive, and possibly even biometric, information about a citizen.

"Some security measures have met with skepticism from the public, such as a proposed national identification card that would provide the government with comprehensive, and possibly even biometric, information about a citizen."

Tighter restrictions on transit travel have also met with frustration and cynicism. After the July 2005 transit bombings that targeted London's underground subway system, for example, officials in New York City took steps to protect the subway there, a difficult task considering that an average of 4.5 million people use the New York City subway every day. But seemingly superficial measures such as random bag checks wasted the time and patience of New Yorkers, and very few of them felt protected by the measures. Because the United States is a free society, the provisions of the searches allowed people to refuse to be searched, somewhat defeating the purpose of catching a terrorist, as he or she could simply decline a search, exit the subway, and reenter somewhere else.

Learning from Israel

To learn how to preserve our open society and at the same time provide a serious level of security, the United States is taking lessons from Israel, a democracy that has lived with terrorism for decades. Indeed, although Israel continues to experience devastating terrorist attacks, experts estimate that Israeli counterterrorism agents intercept more than 85 percent of attempted suicide attacks. Since 9/11, hundreds of U.S. bomb technicians, police chiefs, police officers, and FBI, Secret Service, and Bureau of Alcohol, Tobacco, Firearms, and Explosives (ATF) agents have repeatedly visited Israel for training seminars on how to detect weapons, isolate suspicious persons, and respond to a terrorist attack.

In 2007 the U.S. Transportation Security Administration (TSA) was considering whether to implement an airline security system based on that used by the Israeli national airline El Al. El Al's security is world renowned; according to El Al chairman Israel Borovich, Israel spends twelve times the amount on security per trip that the TSA spends. In addition, El Al's security is handled by the Israeli version of the FBI, called the Shin Bet. Shin Bet agents extensively screen passengers, conducting 10- to 15-minute personal interviews, even flipping through travelers' diaries, wallet photographs, and other items to make sure they are authentic. Though extreme, the high level of security works; despite a slew of enemies, no Israeli plane has been hijacked since 1968.

The USA Patriot Act

One of the biggest debates concerning how to best protect our open society is over the Uniting and Strengthening America by Providing Appropriate Tools Required to Intercept and Obstruct Terrorism Act, otherwise known as the USA Patriot Act. Initially passed after the September 11 attacks and renewed by Congress in 2006, the Patriot Act is a collection of laws that expand the abilities of authorities to investigate and prosecute terrorists.

> **"To learn how to preserve our open society and at the same time provide a serious level of security, the U.S. is taking lessons from Israel, a democracy that has lived with terrorism for decades."**

Some of the Patriot Act's most controversial sections include Section 411, which expands the types of offenses for which immigrants can be deported; Section 802, which narrows the definition of terrorism to potentially include political protests; and Section 201, which grants agents the authority to intercept wire, oral, and electronic communications of citizens. A variety of other provisions allow authorities to access private information about American citizens, such as what books they have checked out from the library and whether they have ever belonged to undesirable political organizations.

The Patriot Act has been hailed by supporters as an important tool with which to fight terrorism and assailed by critics as a dangerous threat to civil liberties and the American way of life. On the one hand, most Americans realize that in the post-9/11 world it is necessary to give up some freedom of expression and movement if it will help authorities apprehend terrorists who would exploit those freedoms to plan and carry out attacks. Indeed, a July 2005 Fox News/Opinion Dynamics poll found that 64 percent of Americans were willing to give up some personal freedoms in order to reduce terrorist attacks.

Furthermore, many argue that the Patriot Act's provisions are minor and do not represent a credible threat to civil liberties. "I have read the act carefully," writes attorney James D. Zirin, "and agree with 99 senators that is a reasonable way to strengthen intelligence and law enforcement against our sworn enemies while doing no significant damage to traditional liberties."[5] Some, such as U.S. appeals court judge Richard A. Posner, believe the hysteria over the Patriot Act signifies that Americans are not yet serious about preventing terrorist attacks. "To the extent that our laws do handicap us in fighting terrorism, it is one more sign that we do not take the threat of terrorism seriously enough to be willing to reexamine a commitment to a rather extravagant conception of civil liberties that was formed in a different and safer era."[6]

> **"The Patriot Act has been alternatively hailed by supporters as an important tool with which to fight terrorism and assailed by critics as a dangerous threat to civil liberties and the American way of life."**

Trading Liberty for Security?

Yet others believe that the Patriot Act represents a slippery slope toward a police state in which citizens' rights to privacy and freedom of expression could be dangerously jeopardized. Senator Russ Feingold expressed this position when in 2001 he cast the only Senate vote in opposition to the Patriot Act: "Preserving our freedom is one of the main reasons that we are now engaged in this new war on terrorism. We will lose that war without firing a shot if we sacrifice the liberties of the American people."[7]

> **Opponents of the Patriot Act complain the government has used the public's fear of terrorism as an excuse to obtain greater control over its citizens.**

Indeed, since the passage of the Patriot Act there have been incidents in which Americans' civil liberties were violated. One such incident involved Brandon Mayfield, a lawyer from Portland, Oregon. In 2004 Mayfield was arrested in connection with the train bombings in Madrid, Spain. According to reporter Nicole Colson, "The government used Section 218 of the Patriot Act to carry out a secret search of Mayfield's home without a warrant. The FBI entered Mayfield's home and copied four computer drives, digitally photographed documents, seized 10 DNA samples and took approximately 335 digital photographs."[8] Mayfield spent more than two weeks in jail before the FBI decided he was innocent of the crime; but by then his privacy had been violated and his reputation tarnished.

In addition to violating the rights of Americans, opponents of the Patriot Act complain the government has used the public's fear of terrorism as an excuse to obtain greater control over its citizens. For this reason, author Fred Edwards warns,

> We need to be constantly awake to the cons and scams that pass as federal security analyses and news reports. After all, these ideas are soon codified into law and common practice. Then we get used to them. Finally, we start to imagine it has always been this way and that living under surveillance is a necessary element of civilization and a natural part of modern life.[9]

As Benjamin Franklin famously quipped, "He who would trade liberty for some temporary security, deserves neither liberty nor security."

It is in this spirit that opponents of the Patriot Act fight for a defense against terrorism that does not require Americans to give up so much of what they believe makes America worth defending.

The Problem of "Homegrown Terrorists"

Compounding these issues was the emergence in 2005 of a new kind of enemy, labeled "homegrown terrorists." These are terrorists who attack from within a culture, such as the bombers who carried out the July 2005 transit bombings in London and some of the agents who plotted in 2006 to down airliners over the Atlantic Ocean. Homegrown terrorists complicate the issues of security, privacy, and how to best prevent terrorism: If terrorists can blend into society and appear as normal members of society, how can they be stopped?

> **"Many experts believe that despite the best defenses, it will be impossible to prevent 100 percent of terrorist attacks or permanently stamp out terrorism."**

The actions of the four bombers who blew up London's buses and subways particularly perplexed the British. Each young man had been born in Britain and seemed, from the outside, to be fully integrated into British society and culture. The men were all in their twenties and, according to columnist Steve Coll, "far from destitute . . . they attended secular state schools and received government and family support throughout their short lives. The ringleader, Mohammad Sidique Khan, even worked for a time at a British welfare agency; later, he was a well-liked teacher's aide."[10]

Some of the bombers were married, some had children; all had strong ties to their work environments, families, and communities. According to the official report on the bombings published by the British government, there was nothing unusual that would have suggested the bombers were any different from their fellow citizens.

> Khan generally appeared to others as a role model to young people; [Shehzad] Tanweer as mature, modest and balanced. [Hasib] Hussain's character did not stand out

> much: extremist doodling on his schoolbook was picked up but it is a long jump from this to identifying a potential suicide bomber. [Germaine] Lindsay, particularly towards the end, appears to have behaved erratically and possibly criminally, but not in a way that aroused suspicion of terrorist intentions.[11]

Can Terrorism Ever Be Eradicated?

The combination of homegrown terrorists and the nature of democratic, open societies begs the question: Will terrorism ever be eradicated, or is it a force that Americans will need to adjust to permanently? Many experts believe that despite the best defenses, it will be impossible to prevent 100 percent of terrorist attacks or permanently stamp out terrorism. Indeed, more than six years into the war on terrorism, many people have resigned themselves to the possibility that the world will simply have to live with terrorism. "The great shock to the American system," writes author Anna Quindlen, "is realizing that no fortress is inviolate, no wall tall enough and no place really safe. Metal detectors, random searches. No toothpaste in that carry-on. Safety is a useful illusion, as modern—and as vulnerable—as a skyscraper."[12]

> **"Others are wary of viewing the problem of terrorism so pessimistically. Terrorism is a reaction to problems in the world, they argue. If these problems can be addressed, terrorism can decline."**

Yet others are wary of viewing the problem of terrorism so pessimistically. Terrorism is a reaction to problems in the world, they argue. If these problems can be addressed, terrorism can decline. During the 1980s when Irish Republican Army bombs rocked Northern Ireland, surely the Irish could not imagine living without terrorism; yet today the IRA is more mainstream than it has ever been, participating in peace talks and legitimate political processes. Authors Ted Lewis and Jason Mark argue that with the right foreign policies, the United States has every reason to expect that terrorism can be a thing of the past. "Imagine Franklin Roosevelt saying that there was no way of turning back the Japanese navy, or Winston Churchill proclaiming that the British would not be able to stop the Nazi onslaught," they argue. "An outcry against this fatalism is overdue. If our officials really believe they cannot stop terrorism, then it is up to the citizens to start looking for leaders who will."[13]

Where Should Fighting Terrorism Fit into America's Priorities?

Opinions differ on how high fighting terrorism should rank in America's national priorities. From some perspectives, antiterrorism efforts must be the nation's first priority because terrorism is an ever-increasing problem. As one editorial written on the fifth anniversary of the 9/11 attacks put it: "With the Taliban making trouble again in Afghanistan, with Iraq on the brink of civil war, with Muslim opinion inflamed against the United States, and with Iran showing no signs of cooperation with US policies, the world seems a far less secure place for Americans than it was on Sept. 10, 2001."[14]

> **"Some believe that fighting social problems, such as poverty, hunger, and disease, can do more to prevent terrorism than engaging in wars and beefing up security systems."**

Others believe that continuing to give terrorism enormous amounts of funding and attention puts the United States at risk from other serious issues. A 2006 *Foreign Policy* poll of more than 100 foreign policy experts and officials, for example, revealed that just 32 percent believed that al Qaeda and terrorism represented the greatest threat to national security. Nearly half of the respondents—47 percent—said that loose nuclear weapons and other weapons of mass destruction developed by rogue nations such as North Korea represent the greatest current threat to the United States. Even more revealing, when asked what deserved to be a higher national priority than fighting terror, the overwhelming majority—82 percent—said that ending

America's dependence on foreign oil should be the United States' single most pressing priority for national security.

Fixing Social Problems to Prevent Terrorism

Still others believe that fighting social problems, such as poverty, hunger, and disease, can do more to prevent terrorism than engaging in wars and beefing up security systems. For example, Pentagon officials are beginning to look to programs that curb the spread of AIDS as one of the best defenses against terrorism. General Charles Wald, the former operational head of the European Command which oversees U.S. military operations in Africa, suggested in 2006 that fighting AIDS should be a leading security priority for the United States on the grounds that the result of millions of people being wiped out by AIDS will be instability, poverty, and desperation that can mutate into breeding grounds for terrorism.

Indeed, at the rate that AIDS is presently killing African adults, 25 million children will be orphaned by AIDS by 2010. Political scientists Susan Peterson and Stephen Shellman believe these children will grow up desperate, disenfranchised, and vulnerable to radicalization. "Does AIDS make war or civil strife more likely? The answer is yes."[15] Such conditions, according to Wald, do as much to threaten national security as weapons proliferation and other concerns. "Where do you think the breeding ground for terrorism will be?"[16] he asks.

Terrorism is possibly the most emotional and multifaceted issue facing contemporary American society. Each year brings changing opinion on how serious the threat from terrorism is, what motivates terrorists to act, and how terrorism can be prevented. As time distances American society from the events of September 11, the issues regarding terrorism become more complicated, and solutions to the problem seem more elusive. To be sure, the topic of terrorism and its many issues—what constitutes it, what motivates it, and how to prevent it—are likely to occupy the nation's attention and resources for decades to come.

How Serious Is the Problem of Terrorism?

"Radical Islamic terrorism is the single greatest threat facing America in 2006."

—Doug Wilson, columnist and chairman of Townhall.com.

"For all the attention it evokes, terrorism actually causes rather little damage and the likelihood that any individual will become a victim in most places is microscopic."

—John Mueller, Ohio State University political science professor.

Since the September 11 terrorist attacks claimed the lives of nearly 3,000 Americans, the problem of terrorism has received much attention. Hundreds of voices contribute each day to the debate over whether terrorism is a real or overblown threat and whether it deserves the amount of time, money, and attention it is given. In order to evaluate the problem of terrorism, it is necessary to explore the scope of terrorism and put terrorist attacks—their frequency, their targets, their success rates—in perspective.

What Is Terrorism?

An old expression states, "One man's freedom fighter is another man's terrorist." Indeed, distinguishing an act of terror from political acts and acts of war can be challenging. Terrorism is surprisingly difficult to define, and determining what qualifies as an act of terrorism has been the subject of countless papers, reports, and studies. One book that covers attempts by the United Nations and other international bodies to define terrorism spans three volumes and 1,866 pages.

Section 2656f(d) of Title 22 of the United States Code defines terrorism as "premeditated, politically motivated violence perpetrated against non-combatant targets by sub national groups or clandestine agents."[17] Terrorism is not always violent; using the threat of violence—a bomb threat against a building, for example—can also be prosecuted as an act of terror. People are not always the target of terrorist attacks; oftentimes only property, such as oil pipelines or animal laboratory equipment, is targeted when a terrorist group seeks to make its point about the world oil market or animal testing.

But terrorism is always intended to do two things: coerce an authority such as a government or corporation into meeting demands, and instill fear in the general population. Indeed, the very simple way of explaining terrorism's goal is that it is meant to terrorize. As researchers Gary S. Becker and Yona Rubinstein write, "Terror takes advantage of people being human and rational. By generating fear, terror, even in the form of a low probability event, may generate substantial effects. Hence, terror generates large scale effect by damaging the quality of our life rather than the 'quantity' of life [that is, how many lives are lost]."[18]

"Terrorism is always intended to do two things: coerce an authority such as a government or corporation into meeting demands, and instill fear in the general population."

What Types of Terrorist Groups Exist?

The United States has designated 42 organizations as foreign terrorist groups that are active worldwide. Among the most prominent are the Abu Nidal Organization, active in Iraq; the Abu Sayyaf Group, active in the Philippines; the Al-Aqsa Martyrs Brigade, Hamas, Hizballah, and Islamic Jihad Group, active in Israel and the Palestinian territories; Jemaah Islamiya (JI), active in Indonesia; the Liberation Tigers of Tamil Eelam (LTTE), active in Sri Lanka; the Revolutionary Armed Forces of Colombia

(FARC), active in South America; to name a few. Currently, the U.S. State Department considers the greatest threat and the most number of wanted terrorists to come from the al Qaeda network, which includes the core al Qaeda organization that perpetrated the 9/11 attacks and numerous splinter groups responsible for attacks in Spain, England, Iraq, Saudi Arabia, and other countries.

The U.S. government also monitors threats from a variety of domestic terrorist groups. Most of these groups are "ecoterrorists," meaning they use extreme methods to protest their opposition to exploitation of the environment or animals. Two of the most active groups in the United States are the Animal Liberation Front (ALF) and the Earth Liberation Front (ELF). The ALF and the ELF have attacked fur companies, mink farms, restaurants, animal research laboratories, and the logging industry. The FBI estimates that the ALF and ELF have committed more than 600 criminal acts in the United States since 1996, resulting in damages of more than $43 million. Some, such as James F. Jarboe of the FBI, warn Americans to remain vigilant against the threat posed by terrorists in their own backyard. Said Jarboe in testimony before Congress: "The FBI and all of our federal, state, and local law enforcement partners will continue to strive to address the difficult and unique challenges posed by eco-terrorists. Despite the recent focus on international terrorism, we remain fully cognizant of the full range of threats that confront the United States."[19]

> **"Although terrorism claims thousands of lives each year, a very small percentage of them are American."**

How Frequently Do Terrorist Attacks Occur?

According to the U.S. State Department, there were 11,111 incidents of terrorism worldwide in 2005, killing, injuring, or kidnapping 74,087 people. Of those attacks, 11,103 occurred outside of America's borders, while almost 30 percent (about 3,500) of all attacks worldwide occurred in Iraq. There were just eight acts of terrorism in the United States in 2005—5 were arsons perpetrated by an eco-terrorist group. No group took responsibility for three other attacks that occurred—an anthrax incident, a school bombing, and an attack on the United Kingdom consulate in New York City.

Although terrorism claims thousands of lives each year, a very small percentage of them are American. According to the U.S. State Department, in 2005 just 56 U.S. citizens were killed in terrorist attacks (the majority of which occurred in Iraq). In other words, Americans accounted for about 0.4 percent of the worldwide total of terrorism fatalities.

"By attacking during a normal event such as having lunch or riding to work, terrorists make people feel unsafe even in the most mundane moments."

With 190 attacks, al Qaeda in Iraq (otherwise known as al Qaeda Organization in the Land of the Two Rivers) was responsible for the most terrorist attacks of 2005 and 55 percent of the worldwide fatalities from terrorist attacks. As of January 2007, al Qaeda in Iraq attacks had resulted in 1,647 fatalities and 3,071 injuries.

Where Do Terrorists Strike?

In keeping with terrorism's goal to frighten, terrorists hit targets that, because they are so ordinary, random, and unavoidable, will inspire absolute fear in people. For example, restaurants have long been a top target of terrorists; diners in Israel, Indonesia, and Russia have all experienced the horror of an explosion going off in a local pizzeria or café. Transportation systems are another top target. Terrorists often choose to strike during morning or afternoon commutes when trains, buses, or subways are likely to be packed with people going about their normal routines. This was the strategy used to blow up four trains in Madrid on March 11, 2004, and again in London on July 7, 2005, when suicide bombers attacked London's bus and subway system. By attacking during a normal event such as having lunch or riding to work, terrorists make people feel unsafe even in the most mundane moments. "Terrorists introduce a small risk of violent death into humdrum daily activities such as taking a bus," writes one author. "Even if that tiny risk is never realized, people suffer from the terror it sows."[20]

In 2005, tourist establishments such as restaurants, hotels, and cafes sustained 351 attacks in such places as Indonesia, Israel, and Egypt, according to the U.S. State Department. Other places that were frequently attacked included police headquarters and government offices, which sustained a combined 2,320 attacks. Most of these incidents occurred in countries such as Iraq and Saudi Arabia and were carried out by terrorists who oppose the war in Iraq. Throughout the Middle East, utilities such as gas or oil pipelines were attacked in 221 incidents, and educational institutions were attacked 185 times. Religious sites, such as temples, mosques, and churches were attacked 176 times, while transportation systems were attacked 140 times.

> **“An attack using a biological agent such as anthrax could kill as many as 130,000 to 3 million people.”**

Is the United States Likely to Be Attacked with Weapons of Mass Destruction?

An increasing topic of discussion since September 11 is whether terrorists might use more sophisticated weapons in terrorist attacks, such as biological, chemical, or even nuclear weapons. Such an attack could kill tens of thousands and destroy critical pieces of American infrastructure. Or would it? There is much debate over whether terrorists could actually get their hands on weapons of mass destruction, and if they could, whether even a carefully planned attack would result in a significant amount of death and destruction.

For some, the threat from a biochemical attack is real and severe. Biological and chemical weapons can be easy to obtain and cheap to make. For example, anthrax, botulism, and strains of the plague are all naturally occurring agents that could be grown and harvested in a laboratory. If dispersed in a subway or city, it could take days, even weeks, to figure out that an attack had been mounted, and by then it would be too late to stop a mass epidemic.

According to an Office of Technology Assessment report prepared for the government, 1,000 kilograms of sarin gas, a chemical weapon, dispersed over a large American city, could kill 300 to 8,000 people. An attack using a biological agent such as anthrax could kill as many as 130,000 to 3 million people. "The unleashing of a living pathogen could be a springboard to a disease outbreak that can worsen over a period of months or years," says bioterrorism expert Leonard A. Cole. "This is especially true if the agent is contagious like the smallpox virus or the plague bacterium, each of which over the millennia have killed hundreds of millions of victims."[21] The threat from biochemical weapons is so severe that former CIA director George Tenet has described "al-Qaeda's program to produce anthrax as one of the most immediate terrorist mass casualty threats we are likely to face."[22]

Is It Worth the Money?

But others say that while a biochemical attack is very frightening, in truth, it would be difficult to properly pull off. Because such agents are unstable and sensitive, they are difficult to weaponize—that is, make potent and stable enough to successfully use in an attack. Climatic conditions such as wind, rain, cloud cover, and temperature, along with the purity of the agent and the quality of the dispersal method, can all interfere with a biochemical attack's success and potency. In fact, in the handful of biochemical attacks that have been attempted in modern history—the 1984 Rajneeshe cult salmonella attack in Oregon, the 1995 Aum Shinrikyo sarin gas attack on the Tokyo subway system, and the 2001 anthrax attacks in the United States—only 17 people have died.

> **"In the handful of biochemical attacks that have been attempted in modern history . . . only 17 people have died."**

In 2004 President George W. Bush approved Project BioShield, which allocates about $900 million to develop antidotes, vaccines, and other precautions against biochemical attacks. But some of America's top scientists say that this level of funding is disproportionate to the threat posed by biochemical weapons. They resent funding being redirected from medical research on, for example, tuberculosis, which kills more than 2 million per year, into research for biochemical attacks, which kill far fewer. As molecular biologist Richard Ebright says, "Bioweapons agents cause, on average, zero deaths per year in the United States, in contrast to a broad range of [other] pathogens that cause tens or hundreds of thousands of deaths per year."[23] Scientists are not the only ones frustrated; as journalist Allison Macfarlane puts it, we are "spending billions of dollars defending ourselves against ghosts, and in the process putting these weapons on a pedestal."[24]

The Nuclear Threat

The threat from nuclear weapons is taken very seriously in both the political and scientific communities. Although most experts agree that terrorists do not have the infrastructure, materials, brainpower, or financing to build their own nuclear weapon, many fear terrorists will acquire nuclear weapons from a nation that is an enemy of the United States, such as Iran or North Korea. Indeed, when North Korea successfully tested a nuclear weapon in October 2006, the immediate worry of politicians, scientists, and citizens was that they would sell their technology to the highest terrorist bidder.

No one debates that if a nuclear attack were to occur, it would be devastating. But there are many who believe much effort is wasted panicking over how bad a nuclear attack would be instead of focusing on whether it is likely to occur. Indeed, a nuclear attack would be complicated and difficult to execute for several reasons. First, there seems to be little incentive for a nuclear regime to give such closely guarded technology away—after all, it makes them vulnerable to a nuclear attack themselves, should relations with the terrorist group sour. Second, nuclear weapons are large, bulky, and unlikely to be easily smuggled into the country. Finally, nations that might be inclined to sell nuclear technology to terrorists do not have very much of it—it is estimated that North Korea has only enough enriched plutonium to

> **"Many . . . believe much effort is wasted panicking over how bad a nuclear attack would be instead of focusing on whether it is likely to occur."**

make a handful of weak bombs. If terrorists were able to use this material against the United States, it would no doubt be devastating; but once the United States determined who sold the terrorists their weapons, it is certain to retaliate—which, considering its vast arsenal of nuclear weapons, would be catastrophic for the country in question. This threat of what is called "mutual assured destruction" has proven to be powerful in preventing armed, hostile nations from attacking each other.

> **Nations such as Libya, South Africa, and Iraq have been deterred from producing nuclear weapons, and the United States and Russia have dismantled scores of nuclear weapons following the end of the Cold War.**

These realities lead many to conclude that for the time being, the United States is not in danger of a nuclear terrorist attack. As author Noah Shachtman puts it, "without the expertise and funding of a state sponsor . . . it's almost impossible to pull off the strike of Biblical significance that the press has been wailing about for so long. Heck, even *with* a state sponsor, it's extremely difficult."[25] Shachtman and others credit the multidecade effort to reduce international nuclear proliferation—the spread of nuclear weapons—with reducing the likelihood that such an attack would come to pass. Indeed, nations such as Libya, South Africa, and Iraq have been deterred from producing nuclear weapons, and the United States and Russia have dismantled scores of nuclear weapons following the end of the Cold War. As military analyst William M. Arkin has put it: "All of the evidence indicates that the threat of nuclear, biological, or chemical war has diminished to a lower level than at anytime in most of our lifetimes."[26]

Putting Terrorism in Perspective

Terrorism is frightening, but it is not even close to being the leading cause of death of Americans or anyone else in the world. Even in 2001, the year when a record number of Americans died in terrorist attacks (2,988 people), more people died that same year from drowning (3,923)—but no one would suggest the United States spend billions of dollars trying to prevent that cause of death. Put another way, even if a terrorist attack were to kill 10,000 Americans, that would still be less than are killed annually in car accidents (about 40,000 per year) and the flu (about 20,000 per year). As political scientist John Mueller has put it, "the number of Americans killed by international terrorism since the late 1960s [including September 11] . . . is about the same as the number of Americans killed over the same period by lightning, accident-causing deer, or severe allergic reaction to peanuts."[27]

"Even if a terrorist attack were to kill 10,000 Americans, that would still be less than are killed annually in car accidents (about 40,000 per year) and the flu (about 20,000 per year)."

Voices such as Mueller's regret that the United States spends an inordinate amount of time and money trying to prevent attacks that in reality harm a very small percentage of the population. While terrorism is a real threat that must be fought against, Bart Kosko, professor of probability and statistics, has put the problem in the following way: "The bottom line is this: There will always be terrorists and legitimate efforts to catch and kill them. But meanwhile, the biggest statistical threat comes from the driver next to you who is talking on a cell phone."[28]

Primary Source Quotes*

How Serious Is the Problem of Terrorism?

"The U.S. remains woefully unprepared for a catastrophic nuclear attack on one major American city let alone six or seven."

—K. Chandler, "Al-Qaeda's Preparations for Nuclear Attack on U.S. Soil Nearing Completion, National Security Analysts Say," *Westside Gazette* (Ft. Lauderdale), vol. 34, no. 29, September 29–October 5, 2005, p. 7.

Chandler is a reporter for the *Westside Gazette,* a Florida daily paper.

"Could terrorists really obtain sufficient materials and put together all of what would be needed to manufacture a nuclear weapon? I'll go out on a limb and say, not after 9/11."

—William M. Arkin, "The Continuing Misuses of Fear," *Bulletin of the Atomic Scientists,* vol. 62, no. 5, September/October 2006, pp. 42–45.

Arkin is a columnist for the *Washington Post* and a military analyst for *NBC News*. He writes frequently that the threat of terrorism is overstated.

Bracketed quotes indicate conflicting positions.

* Editor's Note: While the definition of a primary source can be narrowly or broadly defined, for the purposes of Compact Research, a primary source consists of: 1) results of original research presented by an organization or researcher; 2) eyewitness accounts of events, personal experience, or work experience; 3) first-person editorials offering pundits' opinions; 4) government officials presenting political plans and/or policies; 5) representatives of organizations presenting testimony or policy.

"I'm worried that too many people, both in politics and out, don't appreciate the seriousness of the threat to American security and the evil of the enemy that faces us—more evil or as evil as Nazism and probably more dangerous than the Soviet communists we fought during the long Cold War."

—Joe Lieberman, "Remarks in Waterbury, Connecticut," August 10, 2006. http://lieberman.senate.gov.

Lieberman has been a U.S. senator from Connecticut since 1988.

"Few American politicians or commentators dare to question the conventional wisdom that 'terrorism' is the greatest threat facing America and the world. . . . It is long overdue, but not too late, for the American people to liberate themselves from the aggressive and self-destructive paranoia inflicted on them by unscrupulous abusers of an undefinable word."

—John V. Whitbeck, "'Terrorism': A World Ensnared by a Word," *International Herald Tribune,* February 18, 2004.

Whitbeck is an international lawyer based in Saudi Arabia.

"Terrorism is a rather rare and—in appropriate, comparative context—not a very destructive phenomenon. However, the enormous sums of money being spent to deal with the threat have in part been diverted from other, possibly more worthy, endeavors."

—John Mueller, "A False Sense of Insecurity?" *Regulation,* Fall 2004.

Mueller is a professor at Ohio State University and the author of *The Remnants of War.*

"Intelligence reports based on captured leaders and documents reveal that al-Qaeda is targeting nine U.S. cities with the highest Jewish populations for attack with suitcase nukes and/or multiple dirty and toxic plutonium type radiological weapons."

—Patrick Briley, "Hezbollah, WMD Attacks, Inside U.S. Cities?" *Newswithviews.com,* February 10, 2006.

Briley is a Navy veteran who has testified before the Senate Judiciary, Senate and House Intelligence Committees, and the 9/11 Commission on matters of terrorism.

"The probability of a terrorist attack with an actual nuclear weapon cannot be reliably estimated, and it is surely lower than the probability of virtually any other type of terrorist attack."

—Veronique de Rugy, "Is Port Security Spending Making Us Safer?" working paper #115, American Enterprise Institute, September 7, 2005, p. 8.

Rugy is an adjunct scholar at the Cato Institute. Her research interests include tax competition, financial privacy, bioterrorism, and fiscal sovereignty issues.

"I am more concerned about my safety when I run errands, go out on the weekends or just going to and from work or the grocery store than I am concerned about a terrorist attack. There's a lot of desperation in our community and when people become desperate they are more likely to commit criminal acts or turn on each other. That's the real terrorism."

—Linda Evans, quoted in Arlene Edmonds, "Are We Ready?" *Philadelphia Tribune,* vol. 5, no. 43, September 10, 2006, p. 1A.

Evans is an English professor at the Community College of Philadelphia.

"Bioterrorism may or may not develop into a serious concern in the future, but it is not 'one of the most pressing problems that we have on the planet today.'"

—Milton Leitenberg, "Assessing the Biological Weapons and Bioterrorism Threat," *Strategic Studies Institute,* December 2005, p. 87.

Leitenberg is a bioweapons scholar at the University of Maryland's Center for International and Security Studies. He is also the author of *The Problem of Biological Weapons.*

"It is naïve to think that in today's world of nuclear weapons the USA can fight wars around the world and help other countries like Israel fight wars and not have its own homeland come under attack."

—Dorothy Boulware, "Is the USA Ready for War at Home?" *Afro-American,* vol. 114, no. 50, July 29–August 4, 2006, p. A10.

Boulware is the editor of *Afro-American*, the leading news provider for African Americans in the Baltimore/Washington, D.C., area and longest-running African American, family-owned newspaper in the nation.

"We need to start saying it out loud. Today's terrorism scare is a moral panic—just like the 1950s fear of 'creeping communism,' the 1960s reaction against rock and roll, the 1970s belief that cultists were spiriting away our children, the 1980s anxiety that no child was safe in a daycare center, and the 1990s fear that violent video games were inaugurating a youth crime epidemic."

—Fred Edwards, "The Issue at Hand," *Humanist,* vol. 66, no. 4, July/August 2006, p. 3.

Edwards is editor of the *Humanist* and board chair of Camp Quest, a summer camp for freethinking youth.

"Al-Qaeda's interest in chemical, biological, radiological, and nuclear weapons is strong. Acquiring these is a religious obligation in Bin Ladin's eyes. Al-Qaeda and more than two dozen other terrorist groups are pursuing these materials. . . . For this reason we take very seriously the threat of a chemical, biological, or radiological attack."

—George Tenet, "Written Statement for the Record of the Director of Central Intelligence Before the National Commission on Terrorist Attacks upon the United States," March 24, 2002, p. 32.

Tenet was the director of the Central Intelligence Agency from July 1997 to July 2004.

"The greatest existential threat we have in the world today is biological. Why? Because unlike any other threat it has the power of panic and paralysis to be global."

—Bill Frist, "Remarks to the World Economic Forum in Davos, Switzerland," January 27, 2005.

Frist is a former U.S. senator from Tennessee. He held the position of Senate majority leader from 2002 to 2006. Frist's remarks come from a speech in which he predicted a large-scale biological attack within the next decade.

"The diversion of research funds from projects of high public-health importance to projects of high biodefence relevance represents a misdirection of NIH priorities and a crisis for NIH-supported microbiological research."

—*Science,* "Open Letter," vol. 307, no. 5,714, March 4, 2005, pp. 1,409–10.

The text of an open letter signed by 750 prominent scientists and sent to the National Institutes of Health (NIH) and U.S. lawmakers to protest the diversion of medical research dollars to what they perceive as less important defense projects.

"We have overestimated—grossly overestimated—the terrorist threat. We may be winning a war against terrorism simply because there are few terrorists who are credible threats to the U.S."

—Bart Kosko, "The Terror Threat May Be Mostly a Bluff," *Los Angeles Times*, September 13, 2004, p. B11.

Kosko is a professor of electrical engineering, probability and statistics at the University of Southern California.

"Our offensive against nuclear terrorism should have the highest priority. It should be equipped with all the leverage we can provide it. That's not the case today. And that's why the experts can confidently say: It's only a matter of time."

—James E. Goodby, "U.S. Must Take Offensive Against Nuclear Terrorism," *Baltimore Sun*, February 4, 2007, p. 23A.

Goodby is a former U.S. ambassador and the author of *At the Borderline of Armageddon: How American Presidents Managed the Atom Bomb*.

Facts and Illustrations

How Serious Is the Problem of Terrorism?

- According to the U.S. State Department, in **2005** there were:
  - **11,111** incidents of terrorism worldwide
  - **8,016** terrorist incidents resulting in death, injury, or kidnapping of at least one individual
  - **5,131** terrorist incidents resulting in the death of at least one individual
  - **5,980** terrorist incidents resulting in the death of zero individuals
  - **74,087** individuals worldwide killed, injured, or kidnapped as a result of incidents of terrorism
  - **14,602** individuals worldwide killed as a result of incidents of terrorism
  - **24,705** individuals worldwide injured as a result of incidents of terrorism
  - **34,780** individuals worldwide kidnapped as a result of incidents of terrorism
  - **56** U.S. citizens worldwide killed as a result of incidents of terrorism
  - **17** U.S. citizens worldwide injured as a result of incidents of terrorism
  - **11** U.S. citizens worldwide kidnapped as a result of incidents of terrorism

Terrorists Attacks Around the World

The Near East and South Asia bore the overwhelming brunt of terrorist attacks in 2005.

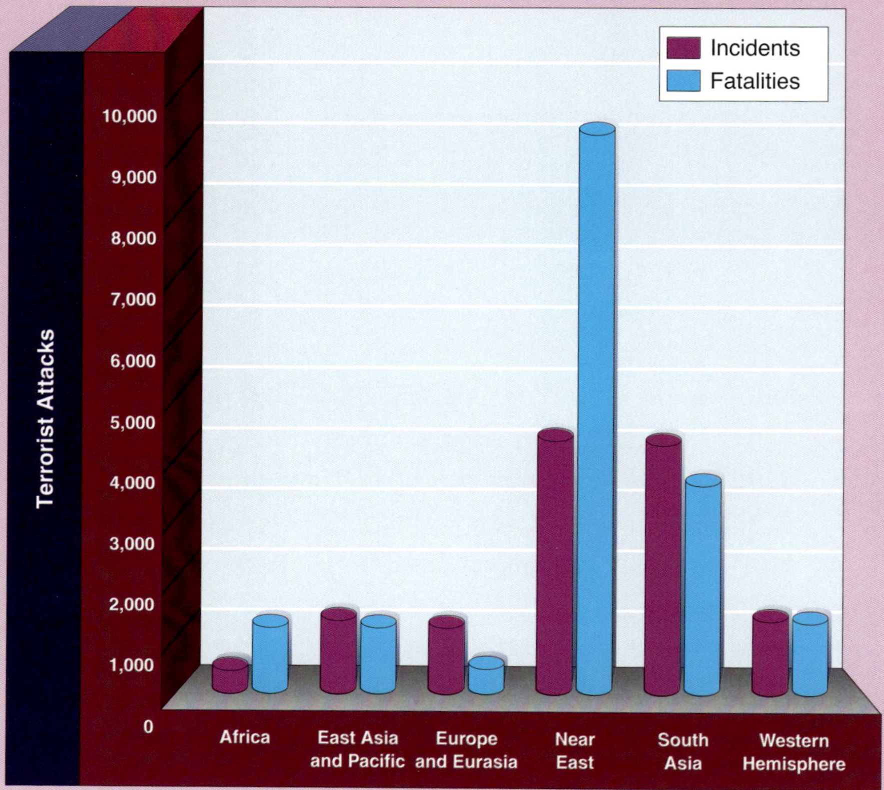

Source: Reviewing the State Department's Annual Report on Terrorism, Hearing before the Subcommittee on International Terrorism and Nonproliferation of the Committee on International Relations, House of Representatives, May 11, 2006.

- Currently there are 8 countries with nuclear weapons, 16 with chemical weapons programs, and **5 to 12** with biological weapons programs.

- The United States spends **$7 billion** on biodefense but less than $2 billion on preventing a nuclear attack.

- The term "weapons of mass destruction" was first used in a **December 28, 1937**, *London Times* article about the German bombing of Spanish cities.

- The United Nations began using the term in 1947, defining weapons of mass destruction as "**atomic explosive weapons**, radioactive material weapons, lethal chemical and biological weapons, and any weapons developed in the future which have characteristics comparable in destructive effect to those of the atomic bomb or other weapons mentioned above."

- In the 2002 National Strategy to Combat Weapons of Mass Destruction, the Bush administration defined weapons of mass destruction simply as "**nuclear, chemical, and biological weapons**."

American Fatalities from Terrorism Are Relatively Low

U.S. Fatalities as a Share of Worldwide Fatalities

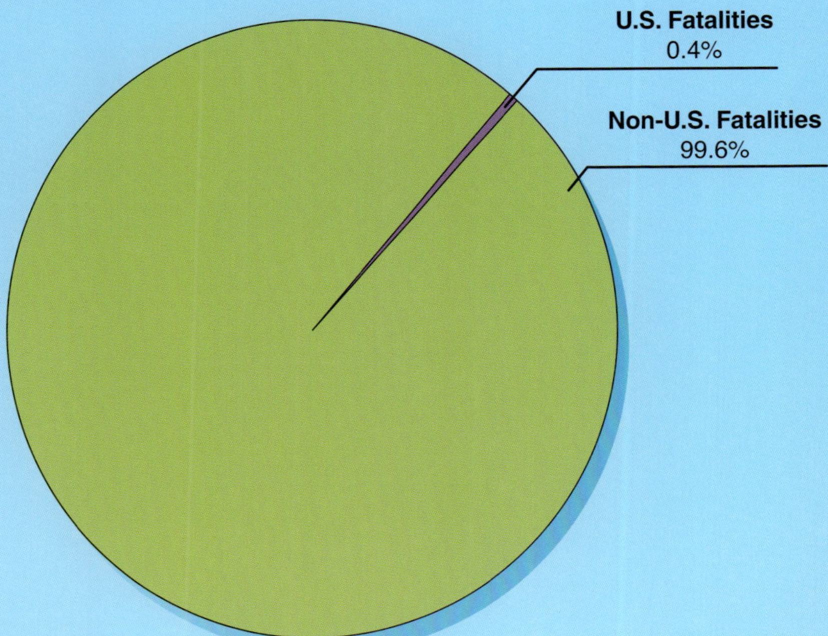

Americans comprise a minority of people killed in terrorist attacks. In 2005, there were 14,602 worldwide fatalities from terrorism and just 56 American fatalities.

Source: U.S. Department of State, 2006.

Expert Opinions About National Security and Terrorism

A 2006 *Foreign Policy* poll of more than 100 foreign policy experts and officials revealed the following attitudes about national security and the threat from terrorism.

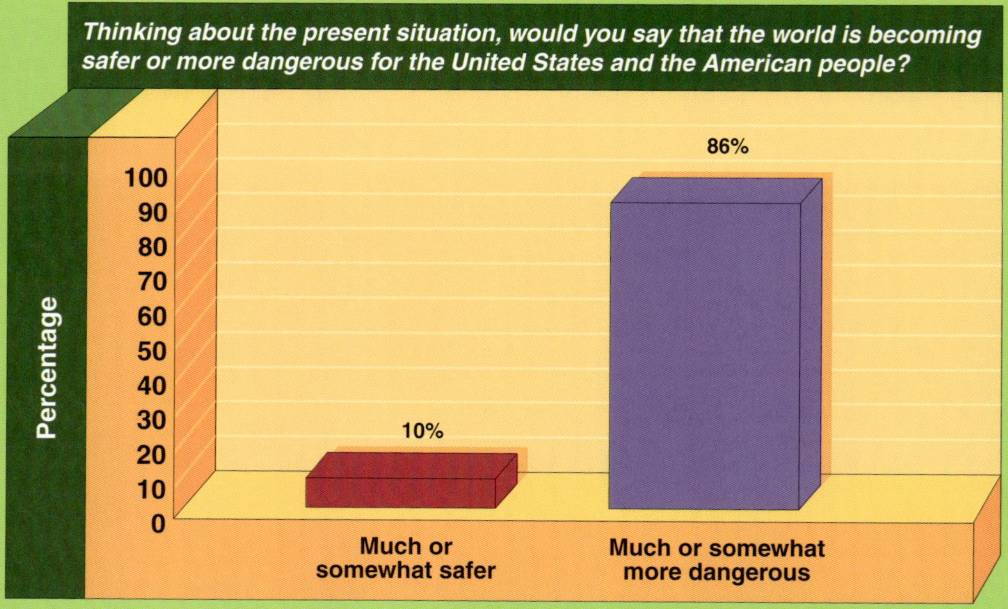

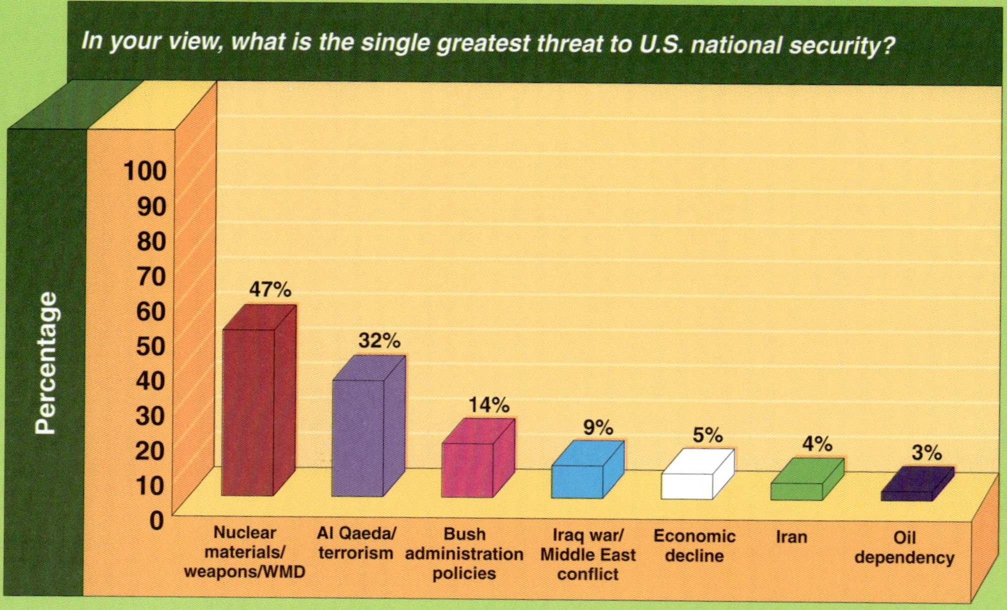

Source: *Foreign Policy* and the Center for American Progress, "The Terrorism Index," July/August 2006.

- The only nuclear weapons ever used in wartime were dropped on Japan by the United States at the end of World War II. The bomb dropped on the city of Hiroshima killed **140,000** people; the bomb dropped on the city of Nagasaki killed **70,000**.

- Modern nuclear weapons average more than **100 kilotons**, or 50,000 times the power of the bomb used in 1995 to attack the Alfred P. Murrah Federal Building in Oklahoma City.

- Since 1900, **40 bio-attacks** have been recorded.

- In 2005 **lighting strikes** killed 90 Americans, while terrorist attacks killed just 56.

- According to a Columbia University poll taken for the five-year anniversary of the **September 11 attacks**:
  - In 2006 just **44 percent** of Americans felt confident that the government can protect their area from a terrorist attack, indicating a downward trend in confidence. In 2005, **42 percent** were confident; in 2004, **53 percent** were confident; in 2003, **62 percent** were confident; and in 2002, **58 percent** were confident.
  - When asked how concerned they were about the possibility of a major disaster or terrorist attack in their community:
    – **61 percent** of the population said very concerned or concerned
    – **39 percent** of the population said not very concerned, not concerned at all
  - When asked how confident they were of the government's ability to **protect public transportation** such as trains and buses from terrorist attacks:
    – **42 percent** said very confident or confident
    – **56 percent** said not too confident or not confident at all
    – **2 percent** said they were unsure

Why Do People Commit Terrorist Attacks?

“The terrorists we face murder in the name of a totalitarian ideology that hates freedom, rejects tolerance, and despises all dissent.”

—George W. Bush, June 28, 2005, speech.

“Contrary to Bush’s claim that we hate freedom, let him explain to us why we don’t strike, for example, Sweden?”

—Osama bin Laden, October 30, 2004, videotape release.

Understanding what motivates people to become terrorists is one of the most fascinating yet frustrating topics regarding terrorism. There are a variety of motivations that drive people to terrorism; these range from an expression of political grievances, to the desire for a homeland, to an outgrowth of religious fanaticism, to a symptom of poverty, despair, hopelessness, and humiliation. Yet, although these explanations are convincing and well documented, in a way, what drives people to kill innocents will always remain a baffling mystery to most moral and humanistic people.

To explain why terrorists act, it is important to examine who they are. To be sure, there is no one profile of a terrorist. Terrorists are male and female; old and young; rich and poor. Though some terrorist attacks are executed by the insane, the poor, and the religiously fanatic, many others are carried out by highly educated, middle-class, rational people who seem, up until the time of their attack, to be perfectly normal members of society.

Terrorists have been husbands, wives, fathers, mothers, sons, daughters, and fully integrated into community activities such as athletic and charitable clubs and organizations. Though their reasons differ, what all terrorists have in common is a desire to express their grievance in a dramatic, shocking, and core-shaking way. One writer explained terrorists' commonality in the following way: "Suicide attackers can be educated and uneducated; religious and secular; comfortably off and destitute; their link is the decision they make to transform their powerlessness into extraordinary power."[29]

To Secure a Homeland

"Terrorists have been husbands, wives, fathers, mothers, sons, daughters, and fully integrated into community activities such as athletic and charitable clubs and organizations."

The majority of terrorist campaigns are carried out in the pursuit of a homeland. What most campaigns have in common—from the assault on Israel by Hamas, Hizballah, Islamic Jihad, and others; to attacks on Turkey and Iraq by the Kurdish KPP; to the Chechen terrorist campaign waged on Russia; to Jemaah Islamiah's attacks on Indonesia; to the Tamil Tigers onslaught of terrorism in Sri Lanka; to Abu Sayyaf's activity in the Philippines—is a specific and strategic goal: "to compel modern democracies to withdraw military forces from territory that the terrorists consider to be their homeland."[30] In each of these places, terrorists believe that a nation wrongfully occupies land that belongs to them. They use terrorism as a military tactic to get the occupying power to cede land so they can create a homeland.

Indeed, Osama bin Laden himself listed the presence of American troops in the holy land of Saudi Arabia as the main rationalization for the 9/11 attacks. In a key fatwa, or ruling, that preceded the attacks, he wrote:

> For over seven years the United States has been occupying the lands of Islam in the holiest of places, the Arabian Peninsula, plundering its riches, dictating to its

> rulers, humiliating its people, terrorizing its neighbors, and turning its bases in the Peninsula into a spearhead through which to fight. . . . We—with God's help—call on every Muslim . . . to comply with God's order to kill the Americans.[31]

In a variety of statements issued since 9/11 and especially since the invasion of Iraq in 2003, Bin Laden and other al Qaeda officials have echoed this sentiment: that they attack the United States and its allies because of their occupation of land in the Middle East.

With this in mind, many argue the key to preventing terrorism is to simply end campaigns of occupation. Writes terrorist expert Robert A. Pape: "Once the occupying forces withdraw from the homeland territory of the terrorists, they often stop—and often on a dime." To this end, experts argue that America's troop presence in the Middle East is a force of provocation that is likely to increase the number of attacks against American civilians. Indeed, Pape is a leader among a growing group of voices advocating the best way to prevent terrorism is to get the United States out of Iraq. "The longer our forces stay on the ground in the Arabian Peninsula," warns Pape, "the greater the risk of the next 9/11, whether that is a suicide attack, a nuclear attack, or a biological attack."[32]

> **"America's troop presence in the Middle East is a force of provocation that is likely to increase the number of attacks against American civilians."**

Protesting American Imperialism

Hand in hand with the pursuit of nationalism is the desire to reduce foreign intervention or influence in a native land. Indeed, there are many people around the world who resent the intrusion of Western, and particularly American, interests into their economies and domestic and foreign policies. From the American perspective, the United States has the right to protect its interests and allies overseas. But from the terrorists' perspective, this presence qualifies as unwelcome meddling that interferes with a nation's right to self-determination.

Anger at such meddling, or what is referred to as imperialism, is increasingly harnessed by those who send terrorists to carry out attacks. Thus terrorists frequently execute attacks on symbols of such influence: Examples include the 2003 bombing of U.S./Saudi apartment complexes in Saudi Arabia; the 2003 attack on a Marriot hotel in Jakarta, Indonesia; the 2004 attack on Israeli tourists in Egypt; the 2005 bombing of three American hotels in Amman, Jordan; the 2006 attack on the world's largest oil processing plant in Saudi Arabia; and many others. Each of these attacks involved targets that symbolize Western economic or political interests, or what deceased al Qaeda in Iraq commander Abu Musab al-Zarqawi had referred to as "backyard[s] for the enemies of the faith" and "center[s] for whoredom and immorality."[33]

> **"The image of the United States overseas . . . [has] attracted more terrorists to the campaign against America."**

Zarqawi's allies see the United States as a bully that preys on weaker and poorer nations. Indeed, several incidents have fostered this image of the United States overseas and attracted more terrorists to the campaign against America. One was the prolonged detention without trial of hundreds of suspected terrorists—some innocent—at Guantanamo Bay military prison in Cuba following the September 11 attacks and war in Afghanistan. Another was the abuse of prisoners at Abu Ghraib and other prison facilities in Iraq, where in 2003 and 2004 inmates were tortured and even killed by U.S. soldiers charged with their care. As a result, writes one editorialist, "many Muslims look at the United States as a jailer and a torturer;"[34] an image which feeds the anti-Americanism that motivates many terrorists. Another author explains how anti-Americanism fuels terrorism in the following way: "Al Qaeda's appeal to many Muslims has more to do with the perception that the United States has become an oppressor than with the particulars of the group's intolerant worldview. This ideological battle is like a judo match in which Al Qaeda turns abuses of power by the United States against its stronger adversary."[35]

Religious Fanaticism

Though it is commonly assumed that religious fanaticism plays a large role in suicide terrorism, there are some terrorist groups that are not religiously driven at all: the Tamil Tigers of Sri Lanka, for example, who usually carry out the most terrorist attacks every year, are mainly comprised of Marxist-Leninist nationalists who do not believe in God. But religious fanaticism clearly plays some role in motivating terrorists. Pape puts the role of religious fanaticism into perspective: "Religion is rarely the root cause, although it is often used as a tool by terrorist organizations in recruiting and in other efforts."[36]

> **Some terrorist groups . . . are not religiously driven at all: the Tamil Tigers of Sri Lanka . . . carry out the most terrorist attacks every year, [and] do not believe in God.**

Indeed, in the pursuit for a homeland or to oust foreign powers from their land, terrorists active in Southeast Asia and the Middle East—including the September 11 hijackers—are motivated by a fanatical religious desire to become a martyr, someone who dies while defending their religion. These terrorists see Islam and Muslim nations as under attack from Western powers and choose to participate as martyrs in an ongoing jihad, or holy war, between what they perceive to be forces of good (Islam) and evil (the West). If they die as martyrs in defense of this cause, they believe they will live forever in a glorious heaven called Paradise.

Many terrorists coming out of the Islamic groups—al Qaeda, Islamic Jihad, Hamas, to name a few—believe that martyrs ride the fast track to Paradise, where a heaven of unlimited food, drink, and sex with 72 virgins awaits them. Raphael Israeli, an expert in the field of Islamic martyrology, describes the heavenly rewards of Paradise as a place where martyrs "can indulge in drink from silver cups, dressed in expensive silk, adorned with silver jewels amidst gardens where wine flows like rivers." Israeli explains the behavior of those who commit suicide terrorism, therefore, "not as a hasty murderous act by a deranged individual" but "as a supreme act by a worthy and chosen individual, who attains in one stroke what the living . . . cannot achieve by a lifetime of good deeds and saintly practices."[37]

"I Am Ready to Die Now"

Looking forward to these rewards, one suicide bomber named Marwan Abu Ubeida described the day he was chosen for a mission as "the happiest day of my life. I can't wait. I am ready to die now."[38] Said one terrorist trainer, Abu Qaqa al-Tamimi, of another terrorist, a young Saudi would-be bomber in his early 20s: "You can't imagine how excited and happy he is. He can't stop smiling and laughing, even singing. He is sure he is going to paradise, and he just can't wait."[39] Scores of letters and videos have been left behind following terrorist attacks in which bombers express similar sentiments: that they carried out their attack in order to become martyrs and be sent to Paradise.

But Muslims overwhelmingly reject the idea that Islam condones terrorism. Voices such as Ziauddin Sardar, an author and professor of Islamic studies, argue that "if suicide killing was a viable weapon of a just war, however conceived, then the Prophet Muhammad himself would have used it. . . . Life is the ultimate gift of God: nothing signifies ingratitude more than taking your own life—whatever the cause."[40]

Sardar and millions of others believe that terrorists who kill in Islam's name have perverted the religion and have brought not heroism, but shame, upon Muslims everywhere.

> **"Millions of [other Muslims] believe that terrorists who kill in Islam's name have perverted the religion and have brought not heroism, but shame, upon Muslims everywhere."**

Does Poverty Cause Terrorism?

A commonly heard explanation for terrorism is that it is a desperate reaction to living in poverty. According to this theory, people who grow up in poor, unsanitary regions and live under occupation are likely to turn to terrorism to express their anger and frustration. Palestinian terrorism in particular is often seen as a reaction to the humiliation, poverty, and despair of existing for decades under Israeli occupation. As psychologist Neil Altman explains, "Believing himself to have already been killed by Israelis, the Palestinian suicide bomber acts to throw his own death back at his oppressor in an act that is at once retributive and communicative."[41]

One person who has articulated a link between poverty and terrorism is Jomo Gbomo, the leader of the Movement for the Emancipation of the Niger Delta (MEND), a terrorist group that seeks to disrupt the oil industry in Nigeria. Gbomo believes that Nigeria's poor living conditions drive Nigerians toward terrorism.

> What we are fighting for needs no explanation. It is there for all to see . . . the living conditions of the people of the Niger delta. How can you explain a situation where we account for all Nigeria's wealth and [yet] we live without electricity in shacks made of cardboard and straw? How can you explain my people drinking from salty creeks in which they bathe and defecate?[42]

Looking for Heroes in Poor Communities

In such places where poverty abounds, young people may also turn to martyrdom as a way to become a hero in their community. Warns Egyptian professor Aleya El Bindari-Hammad, "Unless young people are shown that they have a future of dignity and security and that they have access to decent jobs and can earn a respectful living, some will continue to think that they will find more respect as 'martyrs' for their cause."[43] Indeed, in the Palestinian territories in particular, young people view martyrs as heroes in the way young people in the United States hold firefighters and athletes up as heroes. Their names are praised on posters and street art and in songs and speeches aired on Palestinian television. Writes Israeli, "It is not uncommon to witness

> **"In the Palestinian territories . . . young people view martyrs as heroes in the way young people in the United States hold firefighters and athletes up as heroes."**

hordes of well-wishers coming to the bereaved family of the martyr to express not condolences, but congratulations for the way their relative had paved for them the road to Paradise."[44]

That living under squalid conditions can breed terrorists has not been lost on leaders of the United States, many of whom have, since September 11, supported programs that will improve those conditions. "Deep poverty breeds religious fanaticism and this is the breeding ground that produces the terrorists of today," said California senator Diane Feinstein. "Yet as a country, the strongest, most economically developed, most powerful country on earth, we do so little to eradicate these conditions."[45]

> **"Only 13 percent of Palestinian suicide bombers are from impoverished families."**

Middle-Class, Highly Educated Suicide Bombers

Yet not everyone agrees that poverty is connected to terrorism. A 2003 study by researcher Claude Berrebi at Princeton University, for example, found that only 13 percent of Palestinian suicide bombers are from impoverished families. Additionally, 57 percent of suicide bombers have some education beyond high school, compared with just 15 percent of the population of comparable age. Other evidence that indicates poverty does not breed terrorism is found in the 9/11 attacks—15 of the 19 hijackers were from Saudi Arabia, one of the wealthiest countries in the world, and were raised in middle-class and even rich households. And of course, the al Qaeda leader himself, Osama bin Laden, is a billionaire.

These facts have led many, such as author Salil Tripathi, to reject the notion that poverty causes terrorism. "Think of the millions of poor people who live in abject conditions in Africa and Asia," writes Tripathi. "Many of these countries have experienced strife and violence. But the poor there do not routinely blow up buses or turn their bodies into bombs."[46]

Economics professor Alan B. Krueger's work sheds light on what role poverty plays in terrorism. According to his research, which surveyed international terrorist attacks through 2003, more terrorists do come from poor countries than rich ones but this has less to do with poverty than with a lack of civil liberties in those countries. This is borne out by the fact that not every poor country in the world breeds terrorism; nations such as Mongolia or Ghana are certainly poor but do not have a problem with terrorists. Meanwhile, nations such as Saudi Arabia and Bahrain, which have spawned many terrorists, are economically well off yet lack civil liberties. "The freedom to assemble and protest peacefully without interference from the government," writes Krueger, "goes a long way to providing an alternative to terrorism."[47]

> **More terrorists do come from poor countries than rich ones but this has less to do with poverty than with a lack of civil liberties in those countries.**

Regardless of whether terrorists are poor or not, many seem to share a sense of despair and humiliation that triggers their desire to participate in terrorist acts. This humiliation can stem from a variety of complicated responses to the treatment of Islam, to Western imperialism, to a response to enduring life under occupation or a repressive leadership. Explains El Bindari-Hammad, "Many suicide bombers come from relatively educated, middle-class backgrounds and are not direct victims of material desperation. But they suffer from a desperation no less painful—the conviction that they have been collectively and utterly humiliated."[48]

Primary Source Quotes*

Why Do People Commit Terrorist Attacks?

"Yes, I am a terrorist. Write that down: I admit I am a terrorist. [The Koran] says it is the duty of Muslims to bring terror to the enemy, so being a terrorist makes me a good Muslim."

—Marwan Abu Ubeida quoted in Aparisim Ghosh, "Inside the Mind of an Iraqi Suicide Bomber," *Time,* July 4, 2005, p. 22.

Ubeida is a terrorist-in-training in Iraq.

"Islam [is] the religion of moderation and tolerance that abhors the terrorists who kill innocents in Islam's name, even as Islam is innocent of such crimes."

—Abdullah II, "His Majesty King Abdullah's Address to the Nation Following the Amman Bombings," November 10, 2005. www.jordanembassyus.org.

Abdullah II is the king of Jordan. He gave this speech after terrorists blew up three hotels in Jordan, killing 60.

Bracketed quotes indicate conflicting positions.

* Editor's Note: While the definition of a primary source can be narrowly or broadly defined, for the purposes of Compact Research, a primary source consists of: 1) results of original research presented by an organization or researcher; 2) eyewitness accounts of events, personal experience, or work experience; 3) first-person editorials offering pundits' opinions; 4) government officials presenting political plans and/or policies; 5) representatives of organizations presenting testimony or policy.

“Globalization is a threat to terrorists because it is seen as an artifact of a Western civilization in which the U.S. is at the helm, leading economic and political reform in the Arab world.”

—Audra Grant, in Michael Mylrea, “The Last Safe Place: Lessons from Jordan's Terrorist Attacks,” *Santa Barbara Independent,* December 8–15, 2005, p. 13.

Grant is a political scientist at RAND, a think tank. Her research focuses on the Middle East and issues related to the development of political Islam and terrorism, as well as the attitudinal orientations of Middle East publics.

“For some years now, nearly all terrorists of concern to America's national security and to the quality of life of her citizens have been Muslims.”

—Srdja Trifkovic, “The Jihadist Fifth Column: The Cure,” *Chronicles,* December 2004, pp. 39–40.

Trifkovic is the foreign affairs editor of *Chronicles* and director of the Rockford Institute's Center for International Affairs.

“The idea that the suicide terrorist act is the endeavor of a deranged individual, who is a young male and a fundamentalist fanatic, is totally wrong. The potential suicide terrorist may actually come from different backgrounds, different age groups, be male or female, educated or uneducated, an upstanding citizen or a deviant.”

—Henry Morgenstern, “Suicide Terror: Is Law Enforcement Ready?” *Law Enforcement Technology,* September 2006, p. 32.

Morgenstern is the president of Security Solutions International (SSI), a national homeland security training company that provides awareness training to first responders and others.

"Why would the sons and daughters of commonplace carnage hesitate to visit it upon others, especially those they've come to associate with their misfortunes and to detest accordingly?"

—Anna Quindlen, "A Nation's Fear of Flying," *Newsweek,* August 21, 2006, p. 100.

Quindlen is the author of five novels and six nonfiction books. Her articles regularly appear in *Newsweek.*

"Commentators are eager to offer a bevy of pseudo-explanations—poverty, the Israeli-Palestinian conflict, etc.—while ignoring the motivation the terrorists themselves openly proclaim: Islam. . . . The terrorists are not 'un-Islamic' bandits who have 'hijacked a great religion'; they are consistent and serious followers of their religion."

—Edwin A. Locke and Alex Epstein, "The Terrorists' Motivation: Islam," *Capitalism Magazine,* May 15, 2006.

Locke is a behavioral scientist and senior writer at the Ayn Rand Institute, which promotes Rand's philosophy of Objectivism. Epstein is a junior fellow at the institute. Both specialize in current affairs and the defense of business.

"Those who commit acts of terror, murder and cruelty in the name of Islam are not only destroying innocent lives, but are also betraying the values of the faith they claim to represent. No injustice done to Muslims can ever justify the massacre of innocent people, and no act of terror will ever serve the cause of Islam."

—Islamic Society of North America, "ISNA Denounces Terrorism in the Name of Islam," May 22, 2004.

The Islamic Society of North America supports Muslim communities and works to foster good relations with non-Muslims. Its statement denouncing terrorists who claim to be motivated by Islam was signed by 72 prominent North American Muslims.

“It seems that the Palestinians’ distress from their lives of difficulty and degradation under the occupation pushes many to disdain life and seek the shortest way to the Hereafter, in order to free themselves of reality and reach Paradise.”

—Ashraf Al-‘Ajrami, “Palestinian Authority Columnist on the Causes of Child Suicide Attacks and How to Stop Them,” Special Dispatch Series no. 376, Middle East Media Research Institute, May 6, 2002.

Al-‘Ajrami is a columnist for the Palestinian daily newspaper *Al-Ayyam.*

“Islamic fundamentalism is not as closely associated with suicide terrorism as many people think. . . . If [it] were the pivotal factor, then we should see some of the largest Islamic fundamentalist countries in the world [such as Iran or the Sudan] . . . with some of the most active groups. . . . However, there has never been an al-Qaeda suicide terrorist from Iran [or] from Sudan.”

—Robert A. Pape, interviewed by Scott McConnell, “It’s the Occupation, Not the Fundamentalism,” *American Conservative,* July 18, 2005.

Pape is an expert in suicide terrorism and a proponent of the theory that terrorism is a secular, strategic enterprise to secure a homeland. He has created the world’s first searchable database of every terrorist attack that has occurred since the early 1980s.

“We need to try and understand why people engage in acts that most of us consider immoral, inhuman, and incomprehensible. I think it’s because the perpetrators, correctly or not, perceive themselves to have been the victims of acts equally immoral, inhuman, and incomprehensible.”

—Aleya El Bindari-Hammad, “Defusing the Humiliation Bomb,” *For a Change,* October/November 2005, p. 24.

El Bindari-Hammad is a visiting professor at George Washington University, Centre for International Health. She has also taught at New York University and the University of Alexandria, Egypt.

"Their [the terrorists'] aim is to remake the Middle East in their own grim image of tyranny and oppression—by toppling governments, by driving us out of the region, and by exporting terror."

—George W. Bush, "President Addresses Nation, Discusses Iraq, War on Terror," June 28, 2005. www.whitehouse.gov.

Bush is the forty-third president of the United States.

"America came to spread obscenity and vice and establish its decadence and rebuild culture in the name of freedom and democracy. It hopes to remold the region and change its political, religious, and cultural map according to its personal interests."

—Abu Musab al-Zarqawi, "'Text' of Al-Zarqawi Message Threatening More Attacks," April 6, 2004. www.fas.org.

As leader of al Qaeda in Iraq, al-Zarqawi was the commander of scores of terrorist attacks against American and Iraqi targets until he was killed by the U.S. Army on June 7, 2006.

"Of course, not all Muslims are suicide bombers; it would be ludicrous to suggest that. But virtually all suicide bombers, of late, have been Sunni Muslims. There are a lot of angry people in the world. . . . But the only ones who seem to feel entitled and motivated to kill themselves and totally innocent people, including other Muslims, over their anger are young Sunni radicals. What is going on? Neither we nor the Muslim world can run away from this question any longer."

—Thomas L. Friedman, "A Poverty of Dignity and a Wealth of Rage," *New York Times,* July 15, 2005.

Friedman writes extensively about Islam, the Middle East, and the war on terror in his regular column published in the *New York Times.*

"It is through economics and trade that the insurance industry and other financial services organizations can best help address the causes of terrorism . . . and in so doing directly attack the poverty, hopelessness and anger from which radicalism—that leads to terrorism—so often arises."

—Stephen Patrick Cain, "Trade Is a Powerful Weapon in the War on Terror," *Business Insurance,* vol. 41, no. 6, February 5, 2007, p.12.

Cain is a retired British army major and attorney who consults on counterterrorism.

"To suggest that the poor will become terrorists unless their plight is addressed is gratuitous; worse, it insults them. . . . The poor value life—their own, of their families, and of their neighbors and others around them. Terrorists don't. . . . They [don't] lack material wealth; they lack the sensitivity to value human life."

—Salil Tripathi, "Debunking the Poverty-Terrorism Myth," *Asian Wall Street Journal,* February 23, 2005.

Tripathi is a writer and journalist based in London.

"Any connection between poverty, education, and terrorism is, at best, indirect, complicated, and probably quite weak. . . . There are many good reasons to improve education and reduce poverty in poor countries. Alas, reducing terrorism is probably not one of them."

—Alan B. Krueger and Jitka Malecková, "Seeking the Roots of Terrorism," *Chronicle Review,* vol. 49, no. 39, June 6, 2003, p. B10.

Krueger is a professor of economics and public policy at Princeton University. Malecková is an associate professor of Middle Eastern studies at Charles University in Prague.

"It is within our country's national interest to bring aid and functioning democratic institutions to regions that might otherwise wallow in poverty, involve themselves in religious fanaticism, provide safe havens for terrorists and, yes, ladies and gentlemen, grow a generation of terrorists that will even plague our grandchildren."

—Diane Feinstein, "Global Poverty and the War on Terrorism," speech before the Los Angeles World Affairs Council, March 28, 2002. www.lawac.org.

Feinstein has been a U.S. senator from California since 1992.

Facts and Illustrations

Why Do People Commit Terrorist Attacks?

Terrorism has been practiced by citizens of a variety of countries, including Algeria, Colombia, Egypt, Germany, Greece, India, Ireland, Israel, Italy, Japan, Lebanon, Nigeria, Pakistan, Peru, the Philippines, Saudi Arabia, Spain, Turkey, the United States, Venezuela, and Yemen.

- According to Robert A. Pape's database at the University of Chicago, the only complete collection of **suicide terrorist attacks** from 1980 through 2006:
  - **Two-thirds** of all al Qaeda suicide terrorists are from countries where the United States has had troops stationed.
  - In Lebanon **41** suicide terrorist attacks occurred between 1982 and 1986; the attacks all but stopped after the United States, France, and Israel withdrew their forces.
  - Of the terrorists who committed those attacks, just **8** were Islamic fundamentalists; **27** were Communists and Socialists, and **3** were Christians.
  - Islamic fundamentalists were associated with about **50 percent** of the suicide terror attacks between 1980 and 2003.
  - Of suicide bombers, **42 percent** have post-secondary educations.

- From 1980 to 2003, terrorists waged **18** separate campaigns of suicide terrorism, including those by
  - Hizballah to drive the United States, France, and Israel out of Lebanon

- Palestinian forces to **drive Israel** out of the West Bank and Gaza
- the **Tamil Tigers** to secure a homeland in Sri Lanka
- al Qaeda to oust U.S. forces from the **Arabian Peninsula**
- Chechnyan forces to oust **Russian troops** from Chechnya
- Abu Sayaff to establish a homeland in the Philippines
- the Kurdish KPP to establish a homeland in **Northern Iraq** and Western Turkey
- Iraqi insurgents to oust the **United States** from Iraq

Most Active Terrorist Groups

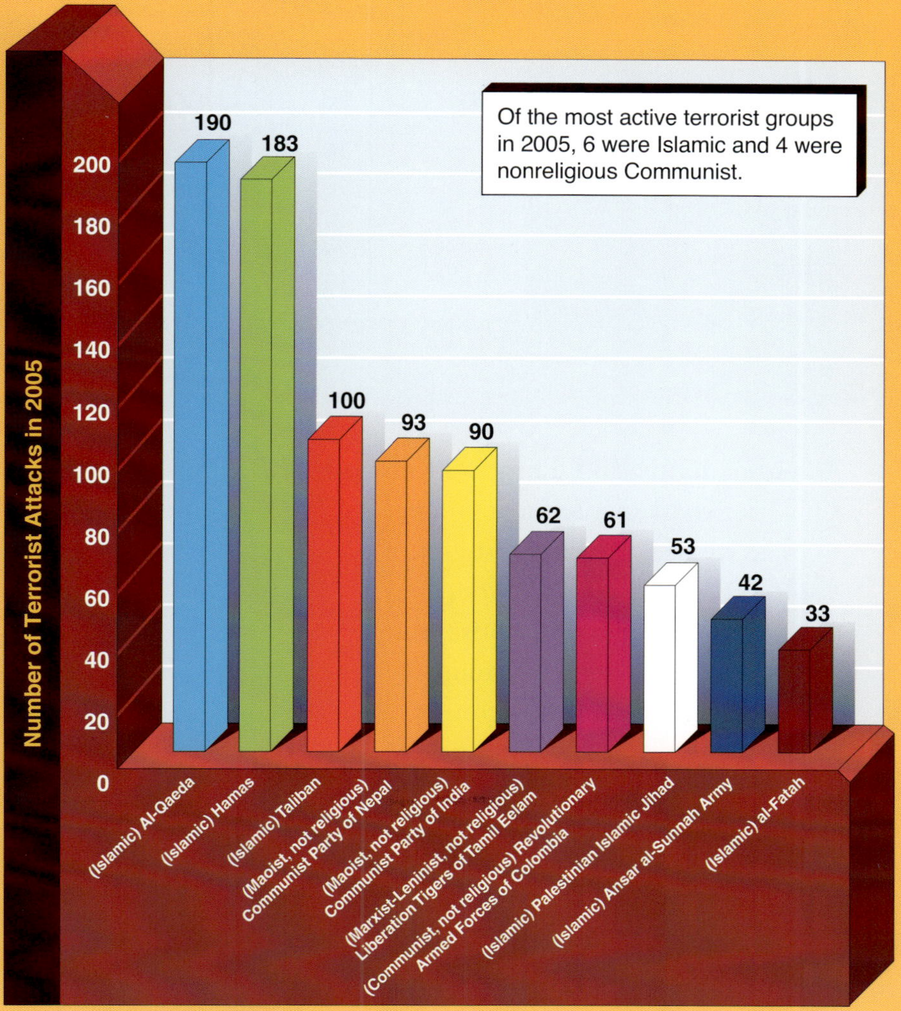

Source: U.S. Department of State, 2006.

Terrorist Activity by Ideology

Since 1968, the following groups have actively committed terrorism. Religiously motivated groups have caused the most injuries and deaths, but Nationalists/Separtist groups have carried out the most attacks.

Group Classification	Attacks	Injuries	Fatalities
Religious	2,652	37,029	13,352
Nationalist/Separatist	4,903	27,253	9,881
Communist/Socialist	3,769	6,830	2,869
Other	299	712	338
Right-Wing Conservative	127	93	275
Leftist	433	337	125
Anti-Globalization	216	98	22
Right-Wing Reactionary	14	10	14
Racist	41	79	7
Environmental	72	42	3
Anarchist	121	16	1

Source: MIPT Terrorism Knowledge Base, March 13, 2007. www.tkb.org.

- According to the **MIPT** Terrorism Knowledge Base, there are:
    - **42** active Islamic terrorist groups
    - **6** active Christian terrorist groups
    - **10** active Sikh terrorist groups
    - **1** Japanese religious terrorist group
    - **1** active pagan terrorist group
    - **1** active Jewish terrorist group

- **Nonreligious** terrorist groups include:
    - The **Sri Lankan Tamil Tigers**, which has committed the most terrorist attacks out of every group in the world; a Marxist-Leninist group opposed to religion

- The **Kurdish PKK**, which is headed by Abdulah Ocalan, a Marxist-Leninist
- The **Popular Front** for the Liberation of Palestine and the al-Aqsa Brigade, which has ties to the Socialist Fatah movement

Most Terrorist Groups Are Nationalist/Separatist Groups

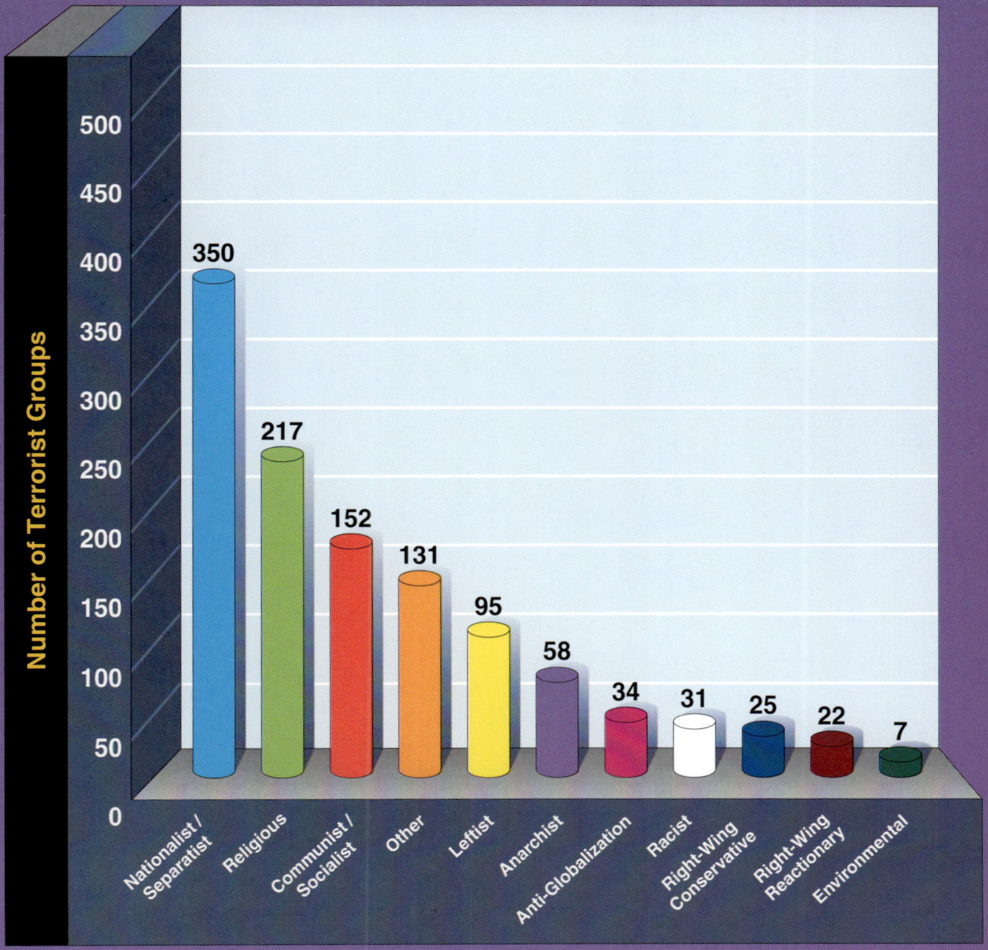

With 350 groups, Nationalist/Separatists make up the most terrorist groups.

Source: MIPT Terrorism Knowledge Base, March 13, 2007. www.tkb.org.

Terrorist Group Origins by World Region

Since 1968, the majority of terrorist groups have originated in Europe, followed closely by groups originating in the Middle East. In that period, there have been 948 terrorist groups.

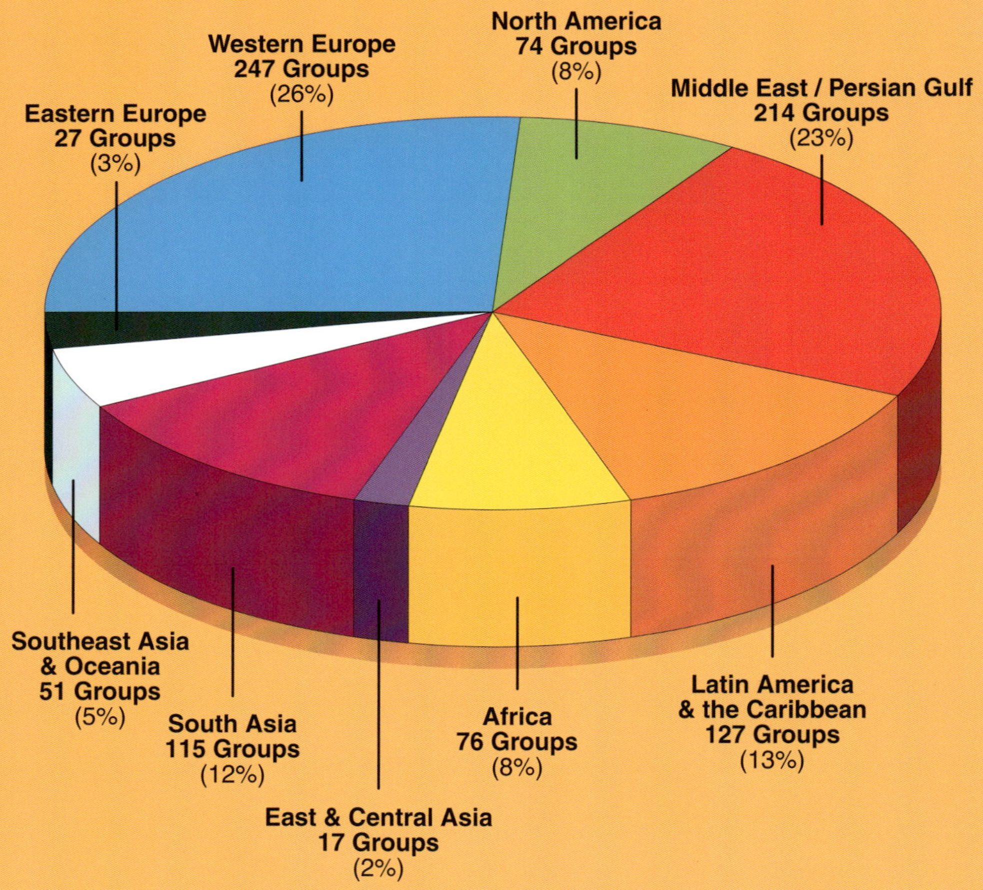

There have been 948 terrorist groups since 1968.

Source: MIPT Terrorism Knowledge Base, March 13, 2007. www.tkb.org.

- According to a 2006 *Foreign Policy* poll of more than **100 experts** and officials:
    - Of the respondents, **80 percent** believe that a widespread rejection of radical ideologies in the Islamic world is a critical element to reducing terrorism.
    - The countries that have produced the largest number of global terrorists are **Saudi Arabia** (62 percent), **Egypt** (13 percent), and **Pakistan** (11 percent). Respondents selected Palestine, Yemen, Iraq, Lebanon, Afghanistan, and Iran each at 1 percent.
    - Of suicide attacks that have occurred in the past 30 years, **81 percent** have occurred since September 11, and the primary motivation for each attack was a military intervention or occupation.

How Are Terrorist Attacks Carried Out?

"Daddy, I want to be a martyr. Can you get me an explosive belt?"

—The nine year-old son of Abu Qaqa al-Tamimi, terrorist handler.

"I ask, on my behalf and on behalf of every father and mother informed that their son has blown himself up: 'By what right do these leaders send the young people, even young boys in the flower of their youth, to their deaths?'"

—Abu Saber M.G., father of suicide terrorist, in a letter to the editor of the London-based Arabic newspaper *Al-Hayat.*

Terrorists use a variety of methods to carry out their deadly plans: Modern-day attacks feature car, roadside, and other types of bombs, known as improvised explosive devices (IEDs); hijackings; shoulder-fired missiles; timed or remotely detonated devices, to name just a few. But the most increasing form of terrorism—and in many ways, the hardest type to defend against—is suicide bombing. Indeed, suicide bombings have all but defined terrorism in the 21st century, and are dramatic, effective, inexpensive, and psychologically damaging. As one editorialist wrote, "There is something novel about the type of terrorism in which the terrorist's death is a necessary and essential part of his act, not just an incidental cost."[49]

But no matter the method used, all terrorist attacks involve careful attention to details and a disturbing level of premeditation. Many of the details about how terrorists execute their attacks are unknown, but what is known is chilling and gripping.

Weapons of Choice

Most modern terrorist attacks are executed using crude, inexpensive weapons—or some, such as the September 11 terrorist attacks, used no weapons at all, save for the box cutters the hijackers used to subdue the passengers on the planes, and the planes themselves. Bombs that are used are usually made of portable materials, such as TNT or chemical compounds made from inexpensive materials. They tend to be small so as to pass through security checkpoints or be easily carried into crowded marketplaces. The July 7, 2005, London transit bombers, for example, made simple chemical bombs that could fit inside the backpacks they took aboard buses.

An increasingly common feature of modern-day suicide attacks is the explosives belt or vest, in which a bomb is physically strapped to the body. Most suicide bombings in Israel, Iraq, Afghanistan, Russia, and other places have been carried out using this device, which tends to be only moderately powerful, killing a handful of people or sometimes just the bomber. To increase the damage inflicted by a minor explosive device, terrorists will sometimes lace it with nails or other debris that increase the number of dead and wounded. Bombs may also be incorporated into a vehicle such as a car or truck and driven into a building or row of stores.

“To increase the damage inflicted by a minor explosive device, terrorists will sometimes lace it with nails or other debris that increase the number of dead and wounded.”

The crudeness of the majority of terrorists' weapons, says terrorism expert Bruce Hoffman, "reflect[s] a recognition of how easy terrorism has become. [Such attacks] are cheap, unpredictable, and difficult to prevent. All that is required is the will to kill and the will to die, neither of which seems in short supply today."[50] Of course, not all attacks require a terrorist to die in the act, and some involve more high-level technology. The March 11, 2004, Madrid train bombings, for example, were perpetrated remotely, killing 191 people and wounding more than 2,000. Terrorists left 10 bombs in backpacks on four trains, each backpack containing about 22 pounds (10 kg) of explosives. The bombs were then detonated remotely by mobile phone. Both remote attacks and suicide attacks require immense strategizing, planning, and preparation, which begin with the recruitment of a terrorist.

Grooming Terrorists at a Young Age

The reasons people decide to join terrorist organizations are many, but each brings a would-be terrorist to the doorstep of a terrorist organization. It is reported that many suicide bombers in the Palestinian territories, Chechnya, and Iraq are walk-in volunteers who rarely have a violent or criminal past. Most experts agree that for many terrorists, especially suicide bombers, "their first experience with violence is their very own suicide-terrorist attack."[51] In each of these regions there are so many people interested in executing attacks that months-long wait lists of would-be terrorists actually exist.

> **"Suicide bombers in the Palestinian territories, Chechnya, and Iraq are walk-in volunteers who rarely have a violent or criminal past."**

Increasingly, those who seek to be terrorists are very young. Oftentimes, young people's ideology and lack of understanding of consequences can be manipulated to make them more willing to carry out an attack. In the Palestinian territories, for example, children are often shown recruitment materials that portray Paradise as a place with toys, candy, and other children happily playing and waving. Eerie voice-overs to such videos say, "How sweet is the scent of the earth, its thirst satisfied by the gush of blood flowing from the body of youth. . . . 'Til we meet, my father, 'til we meet! I shall go with no fear, no tears."[52]

Such recruitment tools work: Young people are executing terrorist attacks in increasing numbers. In 2002 at least 13 suicide attacks on

Israel were either plotted or executed by minors under the age of 18. In March 2004 a group of Palestinian boys ages 12, 13, and 15 were caught trying to sneak into Israel to shoot Israelis in the coastal town of Afula. By 2005 Israeli security forces had arrested more than 50 teenagers for involvement in terrorist activity. March and April 2005 alone saw 15 cases in which teenagers were involved in acts of terrorism, including suicide bombings. Thus it is not surprising that the results of a 2003 poll taken by a Palestinian psychologist revealed that 36 percent of 12-year-old boys in the Gaza Strip believed that the best thing in life would be to die as a martyr in a terrorist attack against Israel.

> **"36 percent of 12-year-old boys in the Gaza Strip believed that the best thing in life would be to die as a martyr in a terrorist attack against Israel."**

"These Are Children Barely 10 Years Old"

Young people are also recruited by other terrorist groups, such as the Lebanon-based Hizballah. According to the Egyptian weekly newspaper *Roz Al-Yusuf,* more than 2,000 children aged 10 to 15 years old have been recruited into Hizballah's armed militias as of August 2006. Writes Egyptian columnist Ashraf Al-'Ajrami, "These are children barely 10 years old, who wear camouflage uniforms, cover their faces with black [camouflage] paint, swear to wage jihad, and join the Mahdi Scouts [youth organization] . . . the children are selected by Hizbullah recruitment [officers] based on one criterion only: They must be willing to become martyrs."[53] Still other young terrorists are graduates from Islamic schools called madrassas, thousands of which are active in Afghanistan, Pakistan, and elsewhere. The September 11, 2001, terrorists were graduates of such schools, along with terrorists who have perpetrated attacks in the Philippines, Indonesia, Russia, and places in Asia.

Although many young people are motivated to become terrorists in order to avenge the death of a brother, sister, or other relative who has been killed by the enemy, frequently people of this type are turned away for fear they will act irrationally, emotionally, or unstable in the moments leading up to an attack. From the terrorists' perspective, it is critical that a bomber not be so emotionally involved that he or she makes a mistake at the last moment. Terrorist organizations look for such qualities in would-be bombers during the recruitment process. As author David Brooks points out, "These organizations do not seek depressed or mentally unstable people for their missions."[54]

"Being organized into cells helps terrorists elude capture and from revealing too much of the terrorist organization's structure and assets should they be caught."

Loosely Connected Terror Cells

Though some terrorists, such as Americans Ted Kaczynski and Timothy McVeigh, work alone, most are part of a larger organization and once they are recruited become organized into cells. Cells are small, decentralized groups of just a few terrorists who are brought together in a particular city or region to carry out a mission. Some members of cells may know each other for many years prior to an attack; others may not know with whom they are working until just days before. Being organized into cells helps terrorists elude capture and from revealing too much of the terrorist organization's structure and assets should they be caught.

One Indonesian government official whose job is to track the Indonesian terrorist group Jemaah Islamiah said, "These people get recruited for jobs and may not even know who or what is recruiting them. Information is kept to a minimum and they are usually only told what they need to know."[55] Indeed, some terrorists know nothing about their attack other than that they will perpetrate one; the date, time, and place are all withheld, sometimes even just hours prior to the attack.

Preparing for a Deadly Mission

Preparing a terrorist for an attack can take weeks or months. One terrorist, who uses the pseudonym Marwan Abu Ubeida, described the typical training and preparation would-be terrorists undergo for their mission. At the age of 20, Ubeida joined an Iraqi insurgency group to protest America's presence in his country. As a suicide bomber volunteer, he underwent a rigorous program meant to discipline and cleanse his mind, body, and soul. This involves reading about the history of jihad (holy war), memorizing fatwas (speeches) issued by Osama bin Laden, and listening to taped sermons of clerics recount what awaits martyrs in heaven.

For inspiration, some would-be bombers visit the sites of previous bombings or watch footage of successful attacks. Others prepare for the experience of death by lying in open graves. Nearly all of them pray. "First I will ask Allah to bless my mission with a high rate of casualties among the Americans," said Ubeida. "Then I will ask him to purify my soul so I am fit to see Him, and I will ask to see my mujahedin [holy warrior] brothers who are already with him. The most important thing is that He should let me kill many Americans."[56]

Ubeida says many terrorists-in-training use their time prior to an attack to pay off debts, resolve family matters, and say goodbye to loved ones. Each compiles a list of 70 people for whom a martyr is permitted to secure a place in heaven, according to Islamic tradition. Some terrorists are elaborately photographed or videotaped with guns, ammo, and Islamic imagery before their death; these are usually released to the media following their attack. Other terrorists, however, prefer to destroy all photos and other personal items just prior to their attack.

> **"Some terrorists are elaborately photographed or videotaped with guns, ammo, and Islamic imagery before their death."**

Terrorist Handlers

Terrorists are typically assigned a handler who helps train and prepare them for their attack. *Time* conducted a rare interview with one such guide who gave his name as Abu Qaqa al-Tamimi. Al-Tamimi's job is to help suicide bombers carry out attacks against U.S. forces in Iraq. He has helped more than 30 of them since September 2004. Al-Tamimi says he provides would-be bombers with safe transit, places to stay, strategic information, weapons, and acts as a guardian, religious guide, and even father figure to them. "Once a volunteer is placed in my care," says al-Tamimi, "I am responsible for everything in his life until the time comes for him to end it."[57]

Handlers such as Al-Tamimi gather intelligence on a target; in Iraq, these tend to be U.S. military bases, Iraqi police stations, restaurants, government ministries, and roads used by U.S. convoys. They notice minutiae that will help an attack maximize casualties; at what time of day a restaurant is most crowded, for example, or when guards change shifts at a checkpoint. "My job is to know how I can get a bomber to the best spot for an attack, at a time when he is sure to inflict the most damage,"[58] says al-Tamimi.

Down to the Last Deadly Detail

After a bomber has been selected for a mission, the handler provides him or her with food, shelter, clothing, and religious texts and inspirational music. While a bomber physically and mentally prepares for the attack, the handler works to arrange the weapon of choice. If it is a suicide bombing, an explosive belt must be procured; if it is a car bomb, a vehicle.

> **"Shazad Tanweer, one of the London bombers, . . . is believed to have carried out a dry run of the July 7, 2005, bombings on June 28 during a trip to London."**

It is also the handler's job to help the bomber do a "dry-run" of the attack—to go through the motions to anticipate any interruption of the plan. Shazad Tanweer, one of the London bombers, for example, is believed to have carried out a dry run of the July 7, 2005, bombings on June 28 during a trip to London. Al-Tamimi helps his bombers get to know the area they will be attacking and helps them learn shortcuts or side streets to anticipate for any sudden changes to the plan. Finally, al-Tamimi frequently hides somewhere in the background to videotape the terrorist act to either learn from it or to preserve the moment for what he says "will one day be part of Iraqi history."[59]

Terrorists in other parts of the world similarly rely on associates who assist them in carrying out their mission. Some terrorists' sole job is to provide support to a suicide bomber or other terrorist, which includes driving them to their destination; providing them with money or clothing needed to carry out their mission; providing lodging; and supplying them with any props or costumes that will facilitate their attack. Male bombers in Chechnya, for example, have disguised themselves in women's clothing to evade suspicion. Other bombers try to blend in as merchants or performers and may carry props to complete the guise. One member of a terrorist group that struck within Israel, for example, was in charge of procuring a guitar for a suicide bomber in order to complete her disguise as a traveling musician.

> **"One bomber, Hasib Hussain, visited a McDonald's just half an hour before he killed himself and 52 other people."**

Maintaining Normality

During the days before the attack some terrorists keep a low profile or even remain in seclusion so they do not arouse suspicion or, for example, get stopped by police for a minor traffic violation. They immerse themselves in prayer and purify their bodies, often giving up smoking or other pastimes. Other terrorists stick exactly to their normal routine so as not to tip off their friends, family, or neighbors.

The July 2005 London bombers, for example, appeared unremarkable right up to the minute of their horrific attack. One bomber, Hasib Hussain, visited a McDonald's just half an hour before he killed himself and 52 other people. Four hours earlier Tanweer reportedly bought snacks at a convenience store and haggled over his change with the cashier. Chilling footage from London Underground security cameras shows the four terrorists chatting and hugging just before they separate, blending into society as everyday, ordinary friends. Maintaining the facade of normality makes even family members unaware of what terrible deeds are about to be set in motion. After the attacks Tanweer's father commented on his son's normal appearance: "Even on the night before he died, he was playing cricket."[60]

Primary Source Quotes*

How Are Terrorist Attacks Carried Out?

“Societies prepare for battle in different ways. Some focus on military preparations, while others focus on prayer. For the Palestinian Authority, battle preparation means encouraging their children to leave their homes for the front lines and to seek death.”

—Itamar Marcus and Barbara Cook, “Seducing Children to Martyrdom,” Teachkidspeace.com, July 4, 2006. www.teachkidspeace.org.

Marcus and Cook are the director and associate director of Palestinian Media Watch, which analyzes and documents the Palestinian media on the Middle East conflict.

“The system of madrassahs has become a hatchery for tens of thousands of Islamic militants who have spread conflict around the world.”

—Benjamin Barber, “Pakistan's Jihad Hatcheries,” *World & I,* vol. 16, December 2001, p. 68.

Barber is a political science professor at the University of Maryland. He writes on matters of terrorism and Islam for *Harper's* magazine, the *New York Times, Washington Post, Atlantic Monthly, Nation,* and has published many books, including the best seller *Jihad vs. McWorld.*

* Editor's Note: While the definition of a primary source can be narrowly or broadly defined, for the purposes of Compact Research, a primary source consists of: 1) results of original research presented by an organization or researcher; 2) eyewitness accounts of events, personal experience, or work experience; 3) first-person editorials offering pundits' opinions; 4) government officials presenting political plans and/or policies; 5) representatives of organizations presenting testimony or policy.

"A nation with child-martyrs will be victorious, no matter what difficulties lie in its path. Israel cannot conquer us or violate our territories, because we have martyr sons who will purge the land of the Zionist filth. . . . This will be done through the blood of the martyrs, until we eventually achieve our goals."

—Na'im Qasim, quoted in Middle East Media Research Institute, "Egyptian Weekly on Hezbollah's Armed Children's Militias," Special Dispatch Series no. 1276, September 1, 2006. http://memri.org.

Qasim is a deputy to Hizballah Secretary-General Hassan Nasrallah. Hizballah is a terrorist group that seeks the destruction of Israel.

"We're making progress in the march of freedom. . . . Today the terror camps have been shut down."

—George W. Bush, radio address, March 4, 2006. www.whitehouse.gov.

Bush is the forty-third president of the United States. He made these comments in a radio address from Asia after visiting Afghanistan, India, and Pakistan.

"Iraq is where the fierce encounters take place, where we recruit and dispatch fighters and where jihad's spirit thrives."

—Abu Zabihullah, quoted in Rod Nordland, "Terror for Export," *Newsweek,* November 21, 2005, p. 38.

"Abu Zabihullah" is the nom de guerre, or war name, of a senior Taliban official who recruits and trains terrorists.

"We must provide an example of moral leadership and devote resources to transforming education in the Muslim world, replacing the odious madrassahs that are the breeding grounds for hate."

—Mortimer B. Zuckerman, "We Can Win—and We Must," *U.S. News & World Report,* September 13, 2004.

Zuckerman is editor-in-chief and publisher of *U.S. News & World Report.*

"When you are willing to die with a bomb that will fit in a backpack, targets like the Jimbaran restaurants [in Indonesia] are basically undefendable."

—Zachary Abuza, quoted in Simon Elegant, "On Terror's Trail," *Time International,* October 17, 2005.

Abuza is the author of several books on Islamic militancy in Southeast Asia.

"There are different types of cells, most notably operational and support. . . . Operational cells will eventually carry out an attack thus revealing their existence if it wasn't previously known. Support cells will remain clandestine even after an attack, and will therefore be much harder to find."

—Jason Belcher, "Destroying Terrorist Cells," *Air & Space Power Journal,* June 24, 2004. www.airpower.maxwell.af.mil.

Belcher is a captain in the United States Air Force.

“Suicide bombing is . . . an interactive, interpersonal act. The suicide bomber is not satisfied with either killing himself alone to make a point (as Buddhist monks have been known to do) or with killing others while preserving himself (as in typical military fashion).”

—Neil Altman, “On the Psychology of Suicide Bombing,” *Tikkun,* March/April 2005.

Altman is an associate clinical professor at New York University and a member of Psychotherapists for Social Responsibility.

“[Suicide bombing] is arguably the most sophisticated weapon available—a human bomb, one that can change its mind, defer delivery, change target or even decide not to deploy.”

—Henry Morgenstern, “Suicide Terror: Is Law Enforcement Ready?” *Law Enforcement Technology,* September 2006, p. 32.

Morgenstern is the president of Security Solutions International (SSI), a national homeland security training company that provides awareness training to first responders and others.

“We have the capacity to be as ruthless and as callous as attacks witnessed in Iraq. We are capable of setting off as many car bombs as we wish and pack them full of shrapnel to maximize casuality. Our fighters can set [oil] rigs on fire with all the occupants onboard.”

—Jomo Gbomo, interview by Brian E. Ross, “ABC News Exclusive: Online Interview with a Terrorist,” January 8, 2007. http://abcnews.go.com.

Gbomo is the leader of the Movement for the Emancipation of the Niger Delta (MEND), a terrorist group that seeks to disrupt the oil industry in Nigeria.

“I have maybe 2,000 mujahadeen [soldiers] in all Iraq, in all towns. . . . If I divide this into groups of 20, I have 100 groups. So this means I have 100 operations in a week. So in a month I have 400 operations. So if in every operation I kill only 2 soldiers, I kill 800 soldiers in a month.”

—Abu Nour, interview by Jill Carroll, “An Interview with an Iraqi Insurgent,” *Christian Science Monitor,* August 22, 2006. www.csmonitor.com.

Nour is a leader of the Iraqi insurgency. He plans and executes terrorist operations and kidnappings. In 2006 he led the capture of journalist Jill Carroll, who was eventually released.

Facts and Illustrations

How Are Terrorist Attacks Carried Out?

- The first modern suicide terror attack occurred in Lebanon on **April 19, 1983**, when terrorists drove a car loaded with explosives into the U.S. embassy, killing 63 people.
- The suicide vest was first invented by the Tamil Tigers for the assassination of former Indian prime minister Rajiv Ghandi in **May 1991**.
- According to a June 2006 *Foreign Policy* survey of more than **100** foreign policy experts, **67 percent** believe that the most likely form of the next attack on American soil will be a suicide bombing.
- The **Mahdi Scouts** organization was founded in Lebanon on May 5, 1985. According to the organization's Web site, as of 2004:
  - Total membership stood at **41,960**;
  - **1,491** young people had undergone training to become terrorists;
  - **120** were ready to become martyrs.
- A 2003 poll taken by Palestinian psychologist Eyad Serraj revealed that **36 percent** of 12-year-old boys in the Gaza Strip believed that the best thing in life would be to die as a martyr in a terrorist attack against Israel.

Teenagers' Involvement in Palestinian Terrorism Increasing

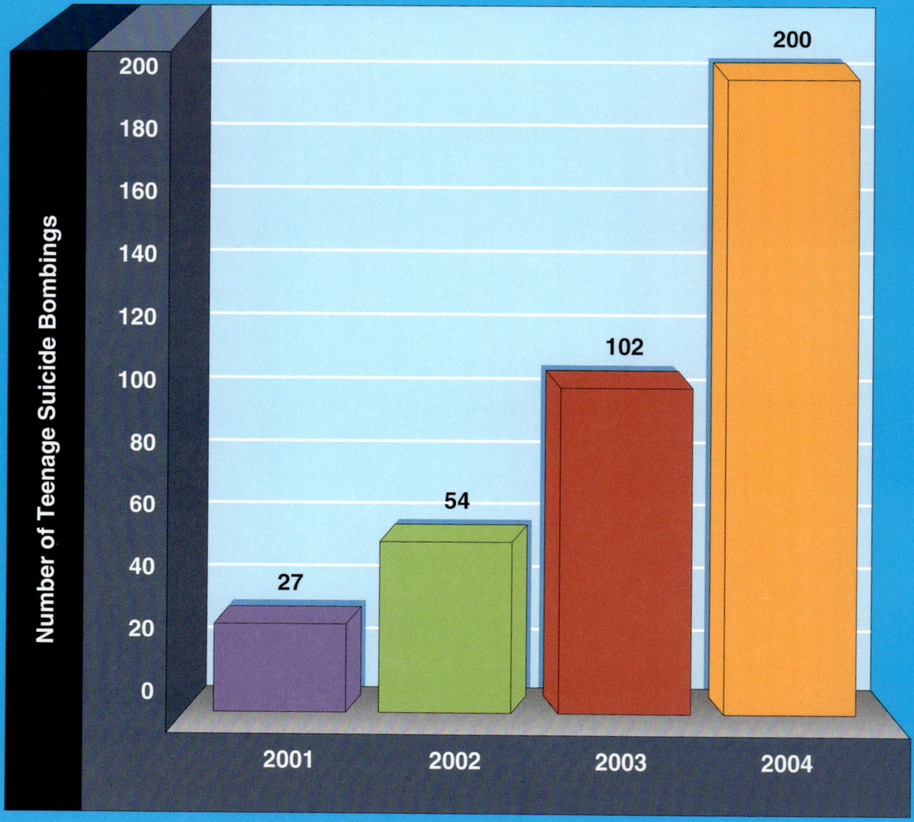

Increasing numbers of teenagers are being recruited by Palestinian terrorist groups to carry out suicide bombings and other attacks on Israel.

Source: Special Information Bulletin, Intelligence and Terrorism Information Center at the Center for Special Studies, June 19, 2005.

- According to the Israeli Defense Forces (IDF):
  - As of May 2005, the Israel Security Agency has questioned **383 minors** for their involvement in terrorism.
  - Since 2005 Israeli security forces have arrested over **50 teenagers** under the age of 18 involved in terrorist activity.

- In April and May 2005, **15 teenagers** under the age of 18 were involved in attempts to carry out terrorist attacks (including suicide bombing attacks) and smuggle arms and ammunition through checkpoints throughout the West Bank.

Using Car Bombs to Kill

Vehicle Description	Maximum Explosives Capacity	Lethal Air Blast Range	Minimum Evacuation Distance	Falling Glass Hazard
Compact Sedan	500 Pounds (In Trunk)	100 Feet	1,500 Feet	1,250 Feet
Full-Size Sedan	1,000 Pounds (In Trunk)	125 Feet	1,750 Feet	1,750 Feet
Passenger Van or Cargo Van	4,000 Pounds	200 Feet	2,750 Feet	2,750 Feet
Small Box Van (14 ft. Box)	10,000 Pounds	300 Feet	3,750 Feet	3,750 Feet
Box Van or Water / Fuel Truck	30,000 Pounds	450 Feet	6,500 Feet	6,500 Feet
Semi-Trailer	60,000 Pounds	600 Feet	7,000 Feet	7,000 Feet

The deadliness of car bombs depends on how large a car is used and how much explosives are packed into it.

Source: Bureau of Alcohol, Tobacco, and Firearms.

- An analysis of suicide bombings in Chechnya, Sri Lanka, Israel and the Occupied Territories, Lebanon, Morocco, Egypt, and Iraq revealed that **34 percent** of such attacks since 1985 have been carried out by women.

- In some instances of car bombs in Iraq, the **disembodied remains** of terrorists have been found with limbs chained to the steering wheel or gas pedal of a car to ensure that the drivers will not change their minds or hesitate at the last minute.

The London Terrorist Bombing of 2005

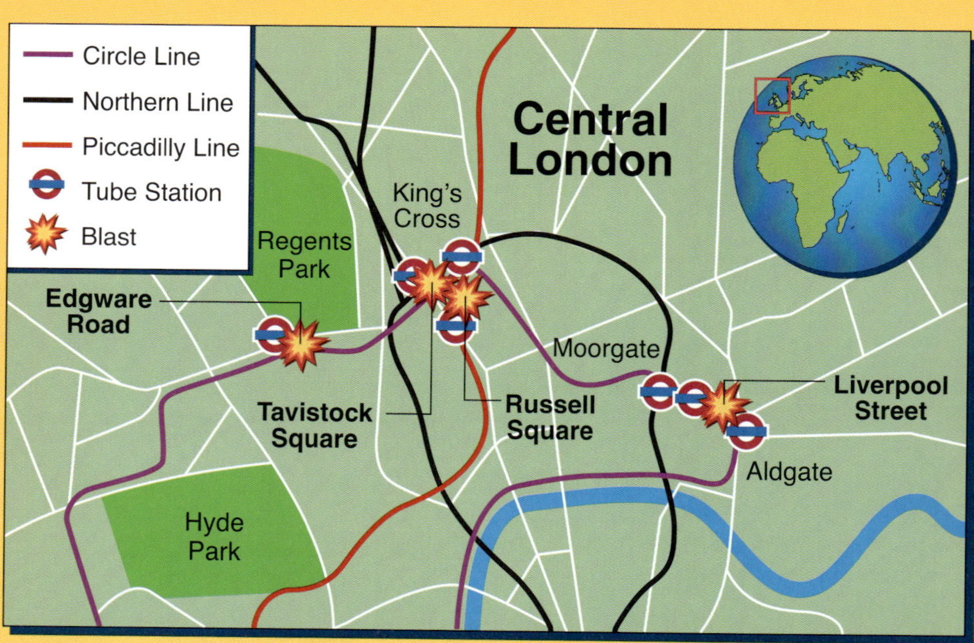

Four bombers split up to explode 4 bombs, killing a total of 52 people. Seven people were killed and 171 were injured between Liverpool Street and Aldgate, 6 people were killed and 163 injured at Edgware Road, 26 were killed and 340 injured between King's Cross and Russell Square, and 13 were killed and 110 injured on a bus in Tavistock Square.

Source: BBC News, "Timeline of the Attacks," BBC.com, July 11, 2006.

What Tactics Do Terrorists Use?

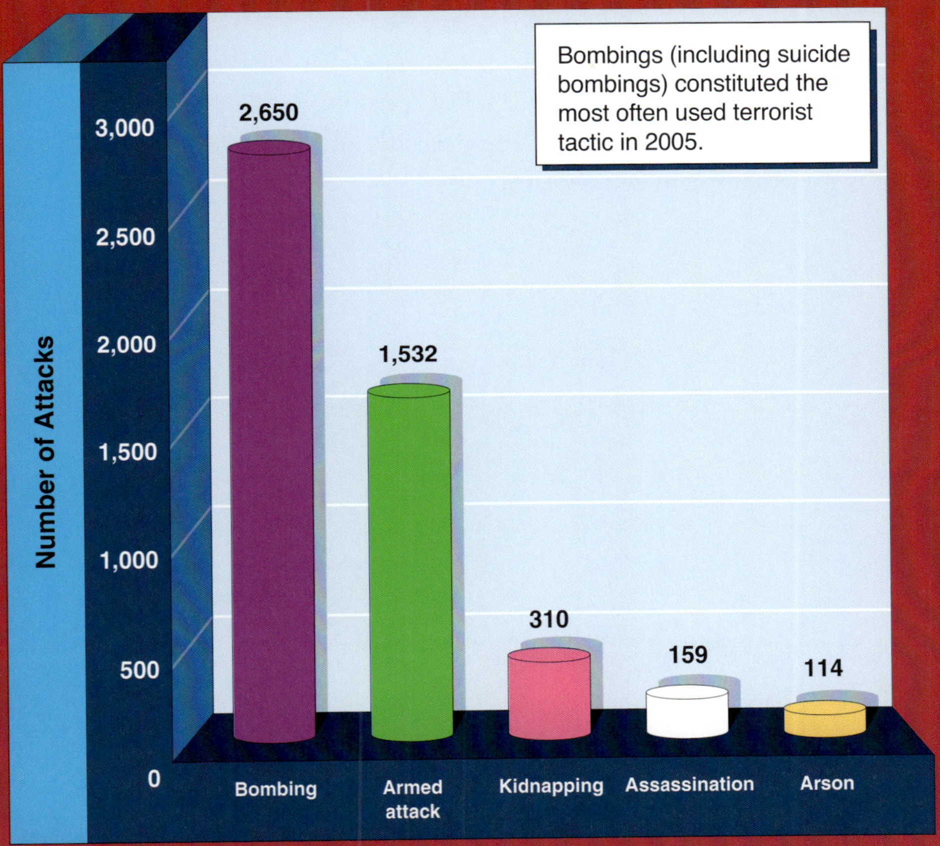

Source: National Counterterrorism Center, *Country Reports on Terrorism*, 2005, Statistical Annex, April 7, 2006.

- According to the Department of Defense, **al Qaeda** operates more terrorist cells than any other terrorist group in the world.

- According to suicide expert Robert A. Pape, who has created the world's first database analyzing terrorist attacks:
    - Nearly all suicide terrorist attacks occur as part of organized campaigns. Of **315 separate attacks**, 301 had roots in organizations involving more people than just the bombers.

- **Suicide attacks** are the fastest-growing type of attack used by terrorists. They have risen from an average of 3 per year in the 1980s, to 10 per year in the 1990s, to more than 40 each year in 2001 and 2002 and **50 in 2003**.

- Suicide attacks amount to just 3 percent of all terrorist incidents from 1980 through 2003, but account for **48 percent** of all fatalities. This makes the average suicide attack 12 times deadlier than other forms of terrorism.

How Can Terrorist Attacks Be Prevented?

"[After] five years of no attacks, five years of successful disruption of attacks, five years of defeating the efforts of al Qaeda to come back and kill more Americans you have got to give some credence to the notion that maybe somebody did something right. We've done a helluva job here at home in terms of homeland security."

—Vice President Dick Cheney, remarks on the fifth anniversary of the 9/11 attacks.

"If there were an attack today, the first responders to a T [subway] attack are, by all accounts, not any better prepared than they would have been five years ago."

—Massachusetts state senator Jarrett T. Barrios, chairman of the Joint Committee of Public Safety and Homeland Security.

There are several different schools of thought on how best to prevent terrorist attacks. Most agree the best way to prevent terrorism is to have a multipronged approach that reflects a bit of each of the following strategies.

Infrastructure and Homeland Defense

One way to prevent terrorism on American soil is to increase security in vulnerable places. Airplanes and airports have received most of the funding available for increasing security; improvements made since 9/11 have included locks for cockpit doors, heightened security measures, and the creation of the Transportation Security Administration, which took over security efforts for all American commercial transportation operations.

Those in charge of securing the nation's skies are always looking to new technologies that will thwart a terrorist attack. Authorities are working on the development of hijack-proof planes that ground-based air traffic officials could take control of and fly to safety. Other inventions include hand-held "electronic noses" that would quickly test passengers and luggage for traces of chemicals and explosives, and passenger-screening devices that would look for suspicious behavior mid-flight. Some experts have advocated equipping planes with antimissile capabilities, an expensive but potentially useful tool, especially after an Israeli passenger plane returning from Kenya in 2002 was narrowly missed by missiles launched from the ground below.

> **"Authorities are working on the development of hijack-proof planes that ground-based air traffic officials could take control of and fly to safety."**

Increased security checks at airports have been the main focus of new security measures. These included testing luggage for explosives with powerful hand-held devices and cross-referencing travelers against a terrorism watch list. However, in 2004 the 9/11 Commission complained that the United States was checking travelers against an incomplete watch list. Furthermore, identity mix-ups often occurred when names were checked. In one embarrassing incident, the famous peace singer formerly known as Cat Stevens was detained by authorities under suspicion of terrorism, because his new name was the same as a suspected terrorist.

Public Safety, Not Headaches

Indeed, many travelers who had shown endless patience following the 9/11 attacks began to view the sometimes senseless and time-wasting security checks with more cynicism. Not wanting to appear as if they were profiling Muslims, airline officials often took an undiscriminating approach to security checks when picking people from a line to be searched—yet everyone agreed that frisking little old ladies for explosives was likely a waste of resources.

The superficiality of these measures led many travelers to feel the government was not taking substantial enough measures toward their safety. "Let's face it," wrote one author, "If we must fear ladies' lip-gloss and tubes of Carmex, the TSA isn't going to keep us safe unless they begin doing cavity searches."[61] While everyone agrees that the TSA should take precautions to prevent another terrorist attack in the nation's skies, Americans have increasingly called for smarter security measures with actionable results. As one editorial board wrote, "The public requires assurance that its government is taking security measures that guard against terrorism, rather than imposing restrictions that bring more headaches than public safety."[62]

Securing a Vast and Spacious Land

In addition to airline security, measures to beef up security in and around nuclear power plants, national landmarks, transit and rail systems, and securing crop duster planes were taken to thwart another terrorist attack. But securing a land as spacious as the United States is no easy task—at more than 9 million square miles, America shares 1,933 miles of border with Mexico, 5,525 miles with Canada, and has more than 12,000 miles of coastline.

The Department of Homeland security has tried to secure these borders by requiring a passport to move through Canadian and Mexican checkpoints instead of a driver's license. Furthermore, a national identification card has been proposed to help monitor who moves across these borders. The national ID card would provide the government with comprehensive, and possibly even biometric, information about a citizen; it has been met with much controversy because opponents worry it would give the government unnecessary access to private information.

> "**Americans have increasingly called for smarter security measures with actionable results.**"

One of the biggest controversies regarding the best way to secure America is happening at her ports. Experts have long worried that terrorists could smuggle a bomb or even a nuclear weapon into the United States via a ship, only a tiny percentage of which are currently inspected at American ports. "Today Customs has only 80 inspectors to monitor the compliance of the 5,800 importers"[63] that send ships into American harbors, writes Council on Foreign Relations expert Stephen E. Flynn. Officials were working in 2006 with a variety of companies to improve America's port security.

Securing America's infrastructure is an incredibly challenging job, making it difficult to assess whether enough can ever be done. On the fifth anniversary of the September 11 attacks, Bush praised Americans for having "tripled spending for homeland security on our airlines, on our ports, and our borders and other critical areas," and pledged to "continue to provide the resources necessary to secure this homeland."[64] But other observers, such as publisher Steven Lasky, are skeptical. "When it comes to protecting our modes of transportation and critical infrastructure," says Lasky, "I still believe we are a disaster waiting to happen."[65]

> **"The Bush administration has pursued [a] terrorism prevention strategy that involves declaring war on nations that harbor or give any kind of financial or tactical support to terrorists."**

War and Nation Building

Since 9/11, the Bush administration has pursued another terrorism prevention strategy that involves declaring war on nations that harbor or give any kind of financial or tactical support to terrorists. After all, the 9/11 terrorists had been trained in terrorist camps in Afghanistan, sheltered there by the former Taliban government. Immediately following September 11, therefore, the United States went to war to oust the Taliban from power, shut down the terrorist training camps, and make a statement to other governments that might choose to support terrorists. Since then the Bush administration made it a priority to go after other regimes that support terrorism, such as Iran and North Korea.

In 2003 Iraq was believed to be a state sponsor of terror. Operating under the assumption that Iraq's leader Saddam Hussein was supporting terrorists and would sell them weapons of mass destruction, the United States invaded Iraq in March 2003. However, since the invasion, no weapons of mass destruction have been found, and Iraq has become a hot spot for terrorism. In fact, according to the U.S. State Department, in 2005 more than 30 percent of all terrorist attacks and 55 percent of fatalities from terrorist attacks occurred in Iraq.

> **Some believe that the presence of terrorism in the new Iraq is just a bump in the long road to bringing peace and stability to a complicated region.**

Some believe that the presence of terrorism in the new Iraq is just a bump in the long road to bringing peace and stability to a complicated region. As Vice President Dick Cheney said about how Iraq has affected the war on terrorism, "I don't know how much better you can do than no attacks for the past five years. . . . The fact is, the world is better off today with Saddam Hussein out of power. Think where we would be if he was still there."[66] Cheney and others believe it will be years before the world can judge the Iraq War as a success or failure. Said former secretary of defense Donald Rumsfeld, the architect of the Iraq War: "Are more terrorists being created in the world? We don't know. The world doesn't know." He called the idea that the War in Iraq has worsened the terrorism problem "nonsensical."[67]

As proof that the War in Iraq has worsened the global terrorist problem, others point to the fact that since the invasion, terrorism worldwide has increased by more than 5,000 percent. Says Paul Pillar, a former national intelligence officer, "With particular reference to the impact of the Iraq war, the unfortunate answer is yes, we are creating them [terrorists] faster than we capture or kill them."[68] A growing number of voices in the government have been inching toward the conclusion that the war in Iraq has worsened the terrorist problem. Indeed, an authoritative intelligence report partially released in 2006, *Trends in Global Terrorism: Implications for the United States,* combined the views of 16 government agencies and concluded that the war in Iraq had unequivocally increased the terrorist threat. As Senator Edward Kennedy put it, "this intelligence document should put the final nail in the coffin for President Bush's phony argument about the Iraq war. . . . The misguided war in Iraq has 'metastasized and spread' terrorism like cancer around the world."[69]

Several prominent senators have joined Kennedy in arguing for withdrawing troops from Iraq in order to get the United States back on track with its original priority: to stem, rather than fan, the flames of terrorism.

> **Terrorist funding [comes] from illegal immigrant smuggling and drugs and weapons sales.**

Crackdown on Terrorist Funding

In addition to incapacitating governments that provide resources to terrorist groups, attempts have been made to cut off other sources of terrorist funding such as proceeds from illegal immigrant smuggling and drugs and weapons sales. Some terrorist groups such as al Qaeda get the bulk of their money from a massive, global fund-raising network that taps charities, nongovernmental organizations, mosques, Web sites, and other private donors.

Al Qaeda takes advantage of the Muslim obligation of *Zakat,* or donating a certain percentage of earnings to charity, to route funds toward terrorist activity. Donations to terrorism may be unintentional; an independent task force on terrorist financing that investigated the problem of charity-funded terrorism found that "some whose donations go to al-Qaeda know full well the violent and illicit purposes their money will further. In other cases, donors believe their money will help fund legitimate humanitarian efforts, but the money is nonetheless diverted to al-Qaeda."[70]

To halt such donations, the U.S. Treasury froze the assets of at least 41 international aid organizations for alleged links to terror groups following the 9/11 attacks, which were believed to have received significant funding from charitable donations. According to the Illinois Coalition for Immigrant and Refugee Rights, the U.S. government closed down 25 Muslim charities and froze $8 million in donations in Illinois alone. After instituting these orders, Bush declared, "Money is the lifeblood of terrorist operations. Today, we're asking the world to stop payment."[71]

Going After Terrorist Assets

Following 9/11 the U.S. government moved to reduce terrorist financing using the same methods they would to stop any large criminal organization: freezing bank accounts and suspicious assets and instituting rigorous anti-money-laundering laws with which banks around the world are forced to comply. Some viewed these efforts as the most critical tool in the war against terror: "As long as al-Qaeda retains access to a viable financial network, it remains a lethal threat to the United States."[72]

But as with other terrorism-prevention initiatives, terrorists are evolving past such measures, and there are indications that the anti-money-laundering and banking laws are no longer relevant to today's terrorism financing campaigns. Terrorist attacks are increasingly low budget and carried out by decentralized terrorist cells that operate small-scale financial fraud schemes such as stealing credit card data and identities, which gives them access to their own cash. "The bad guys are definitely getting smarter," said a European expert on financial crime. "The banking system is so well patrolled they're resorting to more primitive means."[73]

Attacks Getting Cheaper and Cheaper

Reporter Jeffrey Robinson estimates that the 2004 Madrid train bombings, for example, cost less than $1,000 to execute, and the July 2005 attacks in London, around $100. Attacks in Indonesia also seem to reflect this new, low-budget approach; the October 1, 2005, bombings of three restaurants in Bali were conducted by using suicide bombers who walked on foot to their target and blew it up with low-grade, inexpensive TNT. The plot took little money, effort, and planning, compared with previous attacks on hard-to-penetrate targets such as a well-guarded hotel and embassy in Jakarta, attacks that were estimated to have cost $30,000 to carry out. "The attacks suggest that Indonesia's three-year-old crackdown on Islamic terrorists is working, in that the terrorists have been reduced to softer targets, smaller bombs and cruder methods."[74]

> **"The 2004 Madrid train bombings . . . cost less than $1,000 to execute and the July 2005 attacks in London, around $100."**

For this reason, Robinson believes the elaborate laws placed on money laundering will have no effect on the way small terrorist cells finance their operations. "Money-laundering laws didn't stop the bombings in Madrid or in London," writes Robinson, "and they won't stop whatever comes next because terrorists don't need to launder money."[75]

Police Work and Intelligence

Another strategy for preventing terrorist attacks is to use intricate police work and intelligence to unravel plots. Commonly used in European nations and Israel, which have a long history of thwarting terrorism, this method relies on intricate, long-term, undercover investigative police work to foil terrorist plots before they are able to be executed.

One of the most recent examples of successful intelligence work occurred in August 2006, when British Intelligence services thwarted a plot to bring down as many as 10 United States–bound airplanes over the Atlantic Ocean. Using intelligence that had been pieced together for more than a year, Britain's intelligence service MI5 foiled the plot by tying together a vast web of clues in an investigation called "Operation Overt."

Using tips from informers, MI5 began monitoring about a dozen young male Muslims for suspicious activity. They bugged their apartments, tapped their phones, monitored their bank transactions, eavesdropped on their Internet searches and e-mail correspondence, and watched their daily routines right down to where they shopped and did their laundry. Agents secretly installed video and audio recording equipment inside the suspects' apartment and conducted covert searches of the apartment while the residents were out. During one search they found evidence of chemical experiments that suggested plans for making liquid bombs out of commonplace items that might be brought aboard a place.

> **"Long-term, undercover, investigative police work [can] foil terrorist plots before they are able to be executed."**

After witnessing suspects record martyrdom videos, the agents expected the plot was close to being executed. Then, according to Franco Frattini, the European Union's security commissioner, "The plotters received a very short message to 'Go now.'"[76] In a whirlwind of police activity, 25 suspects were arrested and the plot successfully foiled. The success of the British forces was lauded around the world. Richard A. Posner, a U.S. appeals court judge, said the success "revealed the indispensability of good counterterrorism intelligence"[77] and called the method critical to winning the war on terror.

Like the United Kingdom, other nations such as Israel, Spain, Indonesia, and the United States all have extensive counterintelligence operations designed to foil terrorist attacks before they are able to be hatched. Most of the counterterrorism laws enacted by U.S. law enforcement are contained in the Patriot Act, which is covered in the Overview section of this book.

Are We Safe Enough?

> **"Terrorism is a scourge that is unlikely to be 100 percent preventable, no matter how much money, time, and effort is spent trying to defend against it."**

Some believe the combination of the above tactics has allowed the United States to make important strides toward reducing its vulnerability to terrorist attacks. Writes author James Fallows, "Because of al-Qaeda's own mistakes, and because of the things the United States and its allies have done right, al-Qaeda's ability to inflict direct damage in America or on Americans has been sharply reduced."[78] But terrorism is a scourge that is unlikely to be 100 percent preventable, no matter how much money, time, and effort is spent trying to defend against it. As one newspaper pointed out on the 5th anniversary of the 9/11 attacks:

> Are we safer? Of course we are. . . . But 'Are we safer?' is the wrong question. We should be asking, 'Are we safe enough?' The answer to that is, 'Of course not.' And we may never be. . . . No matter how high we build the walls, no matter how intrusive we are in monitoring the comings and goings of individuals, no matter how much we spend on detection devices and border patrols, we can never plug all the holes.[79]

Primary Source Quotes*

How Can Terrorist Attacks Be Prevented?

"Total success against such threats is impossible. Some attackers will get through to us despite our determined efforts and despite any conceivable defenses we mount."

—George Tenet, "Written Statement for the Record of the Director of Central Intelligence Before the National Commission on Terrorist Attacks upon the United States," March 24, 2002, p. 32. www.fas.org.

Tenet was the director of the Central Intelligence Agency from July 1997 to July 2004.

"There is no question that many of our policies have inflamed our enemies' hatred toward the U.S. and allowed violence to flourish. But, it is the mistakes we made in Iraq—the lack of planning, the mismanagement and the complete incompetence of our leadership—that has done the most damage to our security."

—Jay Rockefeller, "Rockefeller Reaction to Declassification of NIE Key Judgments on 'Trends in Global Terrorism: Implications for the United States,'" September 26, 2006. www.senate.gov.

Rockefeller has served as a Democratic U.S. senator from West Virginia since 1985.

* Editor's Note: While the definition of a primary source can be narrowly or broadly defined, for the purposes of Compact Research, a primary source consists of: 1) results of original research presented by an organization or researcher; 2) eyewitness accounts of events, personal experience, or work experience; 3) first-person editorials offering pundits' opinions; 4) government officials presenting political plans and/or policies; 5) representatives of organizations presenting testimony or policy.

"So far the war in Iraq has advanced the jihadist cause because it generates a steady supply of Islamic victims, or martyrs; because it seems to prove Osama bin Laden's contention that America lusts to occupy Islam's sacred sites, abuse Muslim people, and steal Muslim resources; and because it raises the tantalizing possibility that humble Muslim insurgents, with cheap, primitive weapons, can once more hobble and ultimately destroy a superpower."

—James Fallows, "Declaring Victory," *Atlantic Monthly*, September 2006.

Fallows is a reporter for *Atlantic Monthly*. He writes frequently about the war on terror, the war in Iraq, and other issues.

"The NIE [National Intelligence Estimate] is not designed to draw judgments about success or failure. It's an intelligence document . . . it's a snapshot. Look, a success story is when you have democracy successful in Iraq. A success story is when we complete the job. That's the success story. That's the end state that we all ought to reach."

—Tony Snow, press briefing, September 27, 2006. www.whitehouse.gov.

Snow has been the White House press secretary since 2006.

"How safe are we really if the mocha frappacino I purchase beyond the TSA security checkpoint is a terrorist threat?"

—Joseph C. Phillips, "Safe and Secure," *Afro-American Red Star*, vol. 115, no. 3, Sept 2–8, 2006, p. A13.

Phillips is an actor and essayist whose works deal with war, terrorism, and race, among other topics.

"Unlike other terrorist leaders, Osama bin Laden is not a military hero, a religious authority, or an obvious representative of the downtrodden and disillusioned. He is a rich financier."

—Maurice R. Greenberg, "Terrorist Financing: Report of an Independent Task Force," Council on Foreign Relations, 2002. www.cfr.org.

Greenberg is chairman and CEO of American International Group, Inc., and the chairman of the Nixon Center.

"The uncomfortable truth is that Iran plays a great deal and cooperates a great deal with al-Qaeda, far more than Saddam Hussein ever did, and if we want to develop an effective policy to counter Iranian support for terrorism, we are going to have to do more, especially preventing Iran from having nuclear weapons."

—Brad Sherman, in hearing before the Subcommittee on International Terrorism and Nonproliferation of the Committee on International Relations, House of Representatives, 109th Cong., 2nd sess., May 11, 2006. www.foreignaffairs.house.gov.

Sherman is a Democratic Congressman from California. He serves on the Committee on International Relations and the Subcommittee on International Terrorism and Nonproliferation.

"It seems obvious that citizenship, assimilation, religious tolerance—the basic ideals of an open, plural society—should play a prominent part in counterterrorism strategy, to at least complement the funds that governments pour so eagerly into concrete barriers, listening devices, and retina scanners."

—Steve Coll, "Citizens (Talk of the Town)," *New Yorker,* June 5, 2006, p. 27.

Coll is a columnist for the *New Yorker*.

“We use financial tools to make it harder for them to raise money. We’re using diplomatic pressure, and our intelligence operations are used to disrupt the day-to-day functions of al Qaeda. Because we’re on the offense, it is more difficult for al Qaeda to transfer money through the international banking system.”

—George W. Bush, “President Bush Discusses Progress in the Global War on Terror,” September 7, 2006. www.whitehouse.gov.

Bush is the forty-third president of the United States.

“There’s a high probability that [financial] institutions have not learned from Madrid, 9/11 or the London bombings in relation to re-enhancing their systems against terrorist attacks. . . . The increasing costs of compliance and technology are a form of terrorism. We’re damaging ourselves.”

—Graham Dillon, quoted in *Economist,* “Looking for Terrorism in All the Wrong Places,” October 14, 2005.

Dillon is a banking expert with KPMG, a consultancy.

“Frantz Fanon, the 20th century revolutionary, contended that ‘the aim of terrorism is to terrify.’ If that is so, terrorists can be defeated simply by not becoming terrified.”

—John Mueller, “A False Sense of Insecurity?” *Regulation,* Fall 2004.

Mueller is a professor at Ohio State University and the author of *The Remnants of War.*

"By improving security measures for the nation's aviation system, implementing measures designed to protect our critical infrastructure, using biometrics to establish and verify identity, strengthening border security, reflecting the lessons learned from Hurricane Katrina, increasing the nation's preparedness for a disaster, and enhancing information sharing among federal, state, local, and international partners, DHS [the Department of Homeland Security] is leading the effort to protect the homeland."

—Department of Homeland Security, "Protecting the Homeland Post September 11," September 8, 2006. www.dhs.gov.

The Department of Homeland Security was created following September 11, 2001. It combined 22 former agencies into one department charged with preventing terrorist attacks on American soil.

"The fact that we need a new direction in Iraq to really win the war on terror and make Americans safer could not be clearer or more urgent—yet this Administration stubbornly clings to a failed 'stay-the-course' strategy. How many more independent reports, how many more deaths, how much deeper into civil war will Iraq need to fall for the White House to wake up and change its strategy in Iraq?"

—Edward M. Kennedy, "New National Intelligence Estimate Determines That the Misguided War Has 'Metastasized and Spread' Terrorism," statement, September 23, 2006. http://kennedy.senate.gov.

Kennedy has served as a Massachusetts senator since 1962.

“The clearest example of what terrorist operations actually cost came in 1997, when the IRA issued a bomb threat. . . . The damage was measured in millions. The price was a 2 [pence] phone call.”

—Jeffrey Robinson, “Brown’s War Just Doesn’t Add Up: You Can’t Kill Terrorists with a Calculator,” *Times Online,* February 14, 2006. www.timesonline.co.uk.

Robinson is the author of *The Sink: How Banks, Lawyers and Accountants Finance Terrorism and Crime, and Why Governments Can’t Stop Them.*

Facts and Illustrations

How Can Terrorist Attacks Be Prevented?

- The total number of "suspicious activity reports" filed in America on cash transactions more than tripled between 2001 and 2004, surpassing **685,000** in 2004.

- In Britain about **250,000** "suspicious activity reports" are filed each year. The British Bankers' Association estimates that only 3 to 4 percent of the suspicious activity reports filed involve terror financing.

According to the National Counterterrorism Center's *Country Reports on Terrorism, 2005:*

- Iraq accounted for just over **30 percent** of the worldwide attacks (approximately 3500) and **55 percent** of the fatalities (approximately 8300).

- In Afghanistan there were **20 suicide attacks** in 2005.

According to a 2006 *Foreign Policy* special report on terrorism that polled more than **100** of America's Republican and Democratic top foreign policy experts:

- **Eighty-six percent** believe the world is growing more dangerous for Americans despite the efforts of the War on Terror.

- More than **8 in 10** leaders expect an attack on the scale of 9/11.
- More than **two-thirds** say that to win the war on terror, the U.S. policy makers must use nonmilitary tools, such as strengthening the United Nations and other multilateral institutions.
- About **two-thirds** believe that some part of America's infrastructure—a port, train station, or major landmark—will be the next terrorist target.

Thousands of Miles to Protect

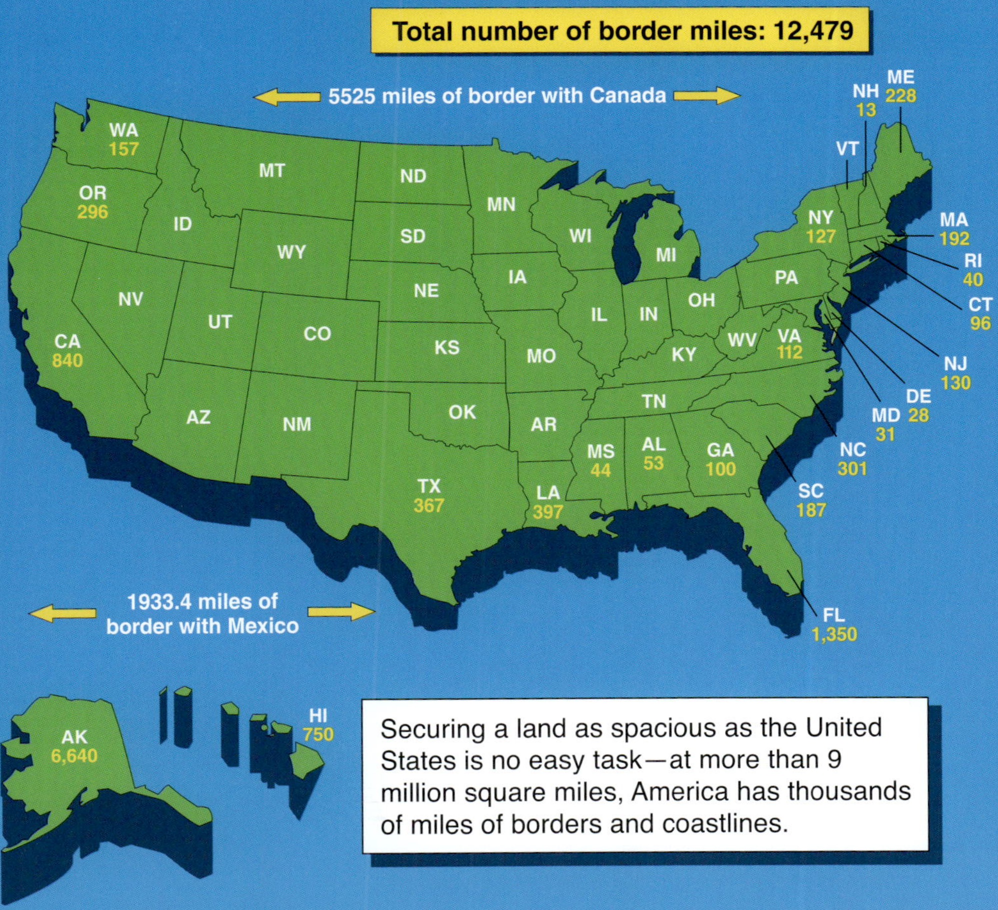

Securing a land as spacious as the United States is no easy task—at more than 9 million square miles, America has thousands of miles of borders and coastlines.

Source: U.S. Department of Commerce, National Oceanic and Atmospheric Administration, *The Coastline of the United States*, 1978.

American Opinions About the Future of the War on Terror

Polls revealed the following attitudes Americans hold about the War on Terror.

America is winning the War on Terror.

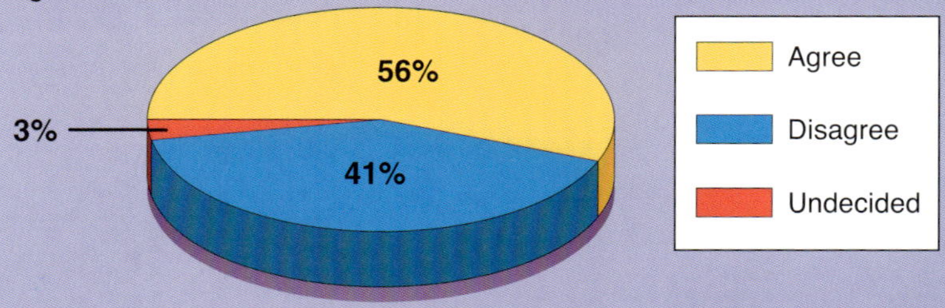

Becoming less dependent on foreign sources of energy will strengthen national security.

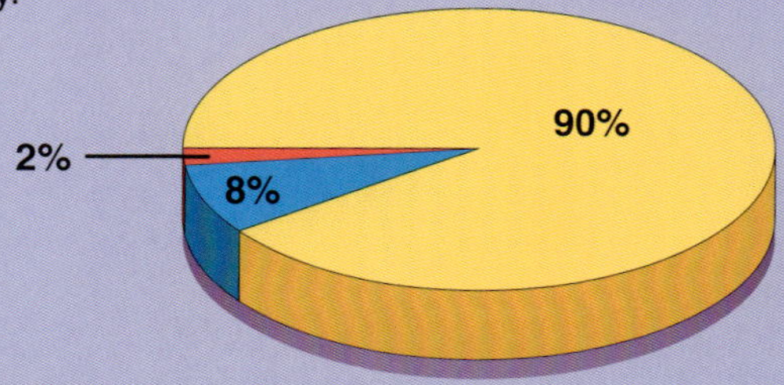

A major terrorist attack is likely to occur in America this year.

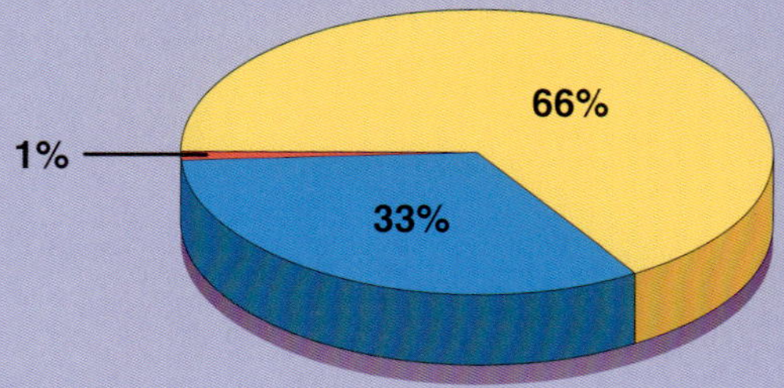

The war in Iraq has had a positive impact on the War on Terror.

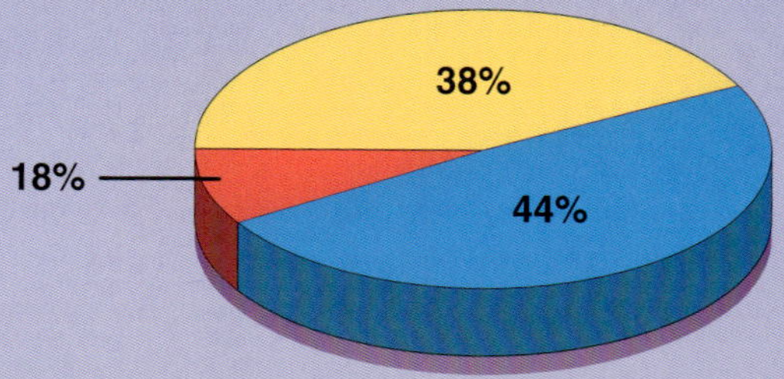

Source: CNN/USA Today/Gallup Poll, January 2006; Harris Poll, February 2006; Pew Research Center for People and the Press, March 2006; CCN/USA Today/Gallup Poll, June 2005.

Grading the U.S. Government on Security

More than 100 foreign policy experts had the folowing views on how to best protect the United States from terrorism. The majority of experts want funding increases for the U.S. Department of State to help it forge more partnerships with other nations to combat terrorism.

Rate each agency's effectiveness at protecting the American people on a scale of 0 to 10.

	Mean Score
Dept. of Homeland Security	2.9
Dept. of Defense	4.4
Dept. of State	4.8
Dir. of National Intelligence	3.9

Indicate whether agencies should receive an increase or decrease in funding.

Percentage of respondents selecting:	Decrease	Increase
Dept. of Homeland Security	19	43
Dept. of Defense	52	15
Dept. of State	7	**87**
Dir. of National Intelligence	13	39

Source: *Foreign Policy* and the Center for American Progress, "The Terrorism Index," July/August 2006.

According to the Department of Homeland Security:

- Each year **$42 billion** is spent on security.
- About **$5 billion** goes toward screening passengers at airports.

Prioritizing the War on Terror

According to a 2006 survey, more than 100 foreign policy experts believe the United States needs to rethink its priorities in the War on Terror.

Please rate the impact of these actions or policies on protecting the American people from global terrorist networks.

Percentage of respondents who selected:	Positive Impact	Negative Impact
War in Iraq	10	87
Guantánamo	16	81
Energy policy	3	64
Iran policy	12	60
Public diplomacy	5	58
North Korea policy	11	49
War in Afghanistan	93	4

Please indicate whether each of the actions listed below should be given a higher or lower priority in the War on Terror.

Percentage of respondents who selected:	Higher Priority	Lower Priority
Reduce foreign oil use	82	11
Improve intelligence	76	1
Stop loose nuclear weapons	68	12
Strengthen the UN	68	12
Strengthen DHS	65	9
Kill terrorist leaders	37	16
Increase military	30	36

Source: *Foreign Policy* and the Center for American Progress, "The Terrorism Index," July/August 2006.

Terrorism Exponentially Increasing Since 2003

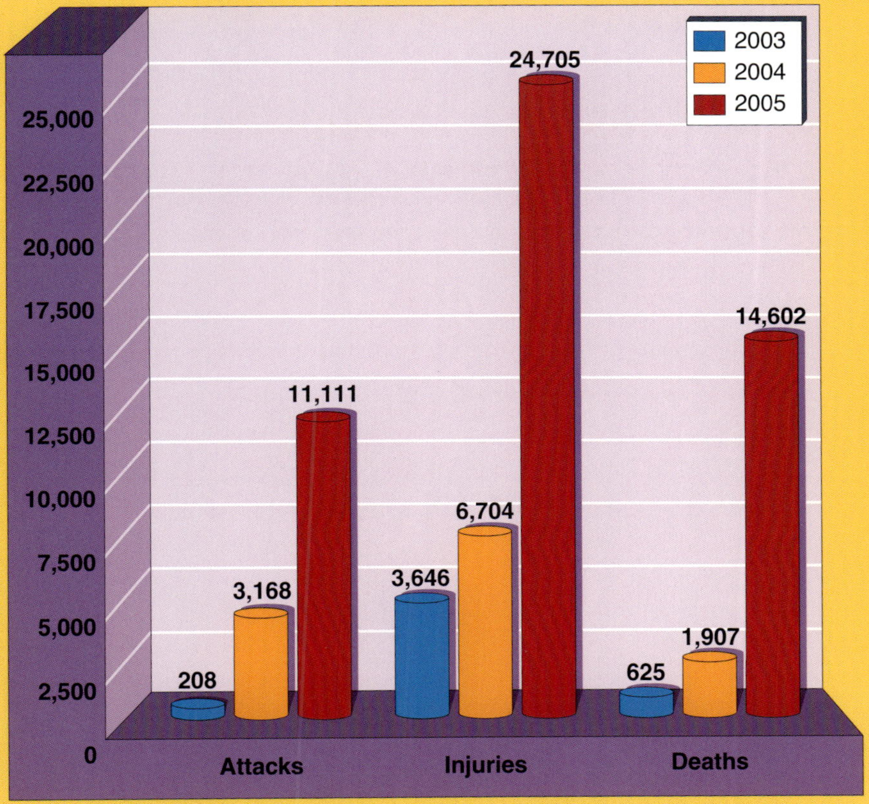

In the three years since the invasion of Iraq, there has been an astonishing increase in worldwide terrorism. Terrorist attacks are up over 5,000 percent and fatalities from terrorist attacks are up 2,000 percent since 2003 when the United States invaded Iraq.

Source: National Counterterrorism Center, *Country Reports on Terrorism*, 2005, Statistical Annex, April 7, 2006.

- The 2007 budget provides **$10.5 billion** for Customs and Border Protection and Immigration and Customs Enforcement to improve border security and immigration enforcement, adding **1,500** Border Patrol agents (an increase of 12 percent over 2006), and **$100 million** for new technology, including portable imaging machines, cameras, sensors, and automated targeting systems that focus on high-risk travelers and goods crossing the nation's borders.

- Department of Homeland Security provides more than **43,000** transportation security officers at over **700** airport security checkpoints and **7,000** baggage screening areas.

- Approximately **4,000** metal and X-ray detectors are present at 440 U.S. airports. The TSA has also deployed 1,200 Explosive Trace Detector machines to passenger screening checkpoints.

- DHS has provided more than **$1.1 billion** to prevent, protect against, respond to, and recover from terrorist attacks, major disasters, and other emergencies.

- In 2006 the eight largest mass transit rail systems in the country were awarded **$103 million** in security grant assistance.

- Since 2001 the number of Border Patrol agents has increased from **9,000** to more than **12,000**, and will double to **18,000** by the end of 2008.

Key People and Advocacy Groups

Al Qaeda: Osama bin Laden's terrorist group. Bin Laden formed al Qaeda in the 1980s to fight Soviet soldiers in Afghanistan. Since then al Qaeda's focus has turned toward fighting the United States. Al Qaeda has splinter groups in various countries in Southeast Asia and the Middle East.

Abu Musab Al Zarqawi: Zarqawi led al Qaeda in Iraq until June 2006 when he was killed by U.S. forces.

Aum Shinrikyo: A Japanese terrorist group that on March 20, 1995, released sarin nerve gas into the Tokyo subway system. Twelve people were killed and more than 5,000 were hospitalized.

Azahari bin Husin: A Malaysian statistician suspected of planning and making bombs for a series of devastating terrorist attacks in Indonesia, including the 2002 Bali nightclub bombing, the August 2003 bombing of a Jakarta Marriott, the September 2004 bombing of the Australian embassy in Jakarta, and the October 2006 restaurant bombings in Bali.

Osama bin Laden: Founder of the terrorist group al Qaeda and mastermind of the September 11, 2001, attacks.

George W. Bush: America's forty-third president. Bush launched the War on Terror following the September 11, 2001, terrorist attacks and also invaded Afghanistan and Iraq under the pretense of fighting terrorism.

Hamas: An Islamic fundamentalist terrorist group that commits acts of terrorism against the state of Israel. Hamas's goal is to achieve a Palestinian state.

Hizballah: An Iranian-backed Lebanese group that commits acts of terrorism in Lebanon and against Israel to protest Israel's existence.

Hasib Hussain: One of the four bombers who perpetrated the 2005 transit bombings in London that killed 52 people.

Saddam Hussein: The former dictator of Iraq. Hussein was deposed by U.S. forces in 2003. He was subsequently tried for war crimes and hanged in December 2006.

Irish Republican Army (IRA): A group that has committed acts of terrorism and guerrilla warfare in order to drive British forces out of Northern Ireland and establish a united Ireland. In recent years the IRA has become more mainstream, participating in peace talks and legitimate political processes.

Mohammad Sadique Khan: One of the four bombers who perpetrated the 2005 transit bombings in London that killed 52 people.

Kurdish Workers Party (KPP): The KPP is made up of Kurds, an ethnic group that lives in northern Iraq and western Turkey. It has committed numerous acts of terrorism in Turkey to achieve an independent state in a region known as Kurdistan.

Liberation Tigers of Tamil Eelam (LTTE): Otherwise known as the Tamil Tigers, this group seeks to create an independent state in Sri Lanka. The LTTE is nonreligious and commits the most acts of suicide terrorism in the world.

Germaine Lindsay: One of the four bombers who perpetrated the 2005 transit bombings in London that killed 52 people.

Nurdin Mohammad: Suspected of helping Azahari bin Husin plan and make bombs for a series of devastating terrorist attacks in Indonesia, including the 2002 Bali nightclub bombing, the August 2003 bombing of a Jakarta Marriott, the September 2004 bombing of the Australian embassy in Jakarta, and the October 2006 restaurant bombings in Bali.

Robert A. Pape: American political scientist known for his work on international security affairs, especially suicide terrorism. Pape compiled the first database of suicide terrorist attacks and, using his data, has argued that suicide bombing is not a fanatical phenomenon but a strategic tactic to get an occupying power to leave land. He is currently a professor of political science at the University of Chicago.

Donald Rumsfeld: Bush administration secretary of defense from 2000 to 2006 and architect of the Iraq War.

The Taliban: The former Islamic fundamentalist government in Afghanistan. The Taliban were ousted from power in 2001 by U.S. forces after refusing to turn over Osama bin Laden.

Shehzad Tanweer: One of the four bombers who perpetrated the 2005 transit bombings in London that killed 52 people.

Chronology

1979
The Soviet army invades Afghanistan; Osama bin Laden (OBL) heads to the region to fight.

1980s
OBL creates al Qaeda, which in Arabic translates as the "base" or "foundation."

1987
First Palestinian Intifada, or uprising, against Israel begins; it features small-scale terrorist attacks.

1990
August: Iraq invades Kuwait. Saudi Government agrees to allow U.S. troops to be stationed in the Kingdom for 1st Gulf War. OBL fiercely opposes troop presence on Islamic holy land.

Early 1990s
Violence occurs in a number of regions worldwide, including Afghanistan, Egypt, Algeria, Libya, Chechnya, Bosnia, Tajikistan, East Africa, Yemen, and the Philippines. Groups that will become significant international terrorist players form, including Libyan Islamic Fighting Group and Abu Sayaff.

1991
Al Qaeda evolves from a paramilitary organization to a terrorist group, focusing on ousting the United States from the Arabian Peninsula. First Palestinian Intifada ends.

1992
Terrorists attack hotels hosting U.S. troops in Somalia.

1993
February 26: Terrorist Ramzi Yousef detonates explosives in the underground garage of the World Trade Center.

1994
Taliban established.

1996
Al Qaeda leadership moves to Afghanistan, establishes training camps for terrorists. OBL publishes fatwa "Declaration of War Against the Americans Occupying the Land of the Two Holy Places."

1997
Islamic gunmen attack tourists in Luxor, Egypt, in November.

1998
February: OBL publishes a second fatwa calling for jihad "to kill the Americans and their allies—civilian and military."

August: Al Qaeda bombs U.S. embassies in Tanzania and Kenya.

December: Sixteen tourists are kidnapped in Yemen.

1999
December: Indian airlines flight hijacked by terrorists seeking independence for Kashmir.

2000
Second Palestinian Intifada, or Al-Aqsa Intifada, begins. Features routine suicide bombings of Israeli checkpoints, cafés, restaurants, hotels, and markets.

October: Al Qaeda terrorists bomb the USS *Cole* in Aden, killing 17 sailors.

1980 1984 1988 1992 1996 2000

2001
September: Al Qaeda operatives crash hijacked airliners into the World Trade Center, the Pentagon, and a field in Pennsylvania.

October: The U.S. leads a coalition to expel the Taliban and al Qaeda leadership from Afghanistan and dismantle leadership; terrorist assets are frozen worldwide. Kashmir Assembly in India attacked by militants.

December: Militants attack Indian Parliament in New Delhi. Plans to attack U.S., Australian, and British Missions in Singapore are thwarted. Terrorist Richard Reid attempts to blow up a U.S. plane with explosives packed in his shoes.

2003
March: The U.S. invades Iraq.

May–November: Terrorists attack residential compounds in Riyadh, Saudi Arabia.

May: Terrorists attack various Jewish targets in Casablanca, Morocco.

August: Terrorists attack Marriott Hotel in Jakarta, Indonesia.

November: Terrorists attack Jewish and British targets in Istanbul, Turkey.

2006
August: British authorities thwart a plot to blow up as many as 10 airliners over the Atlantic Ocean.

2002 2003 2004 2005 2006 2007

2004
February: Bomb explodes on the Superferry in Manila, Philippines.

March: Terrorists blow up four trains in Madrid, Spain, killing 191. Spanish forces are subsequently pulled out of Iraq.

May: Terrorists attack multiple sites in Al Khobar, Saudi Arabia.

August: Chechen terrorists down two passenger aircraft over Russia.

September: Suicide bombing on the Moscow metro; terrorists take more than 1,000 hostage at a school in North Ossetia. Terrorists attack the Australian embassy in Jakarta, Indonesia.

2007
January: Terrorists blow up a hotel and newspaper office in Bangkok, Thailand.

2005
March: A Western theater in Qatar is suicide-bombed.

April: Bomb is detonated in Cairo bazaar alongside other suicide attacks against tourists in Egypt.

July: Terrorists blow up trains and buses in London, killing 52.

October: Terrorists strike multiple restaurants in Bali.

2002
April: Western tourists are attacked at a synagogue in Tunisia.

May: Attack against a bus transporting French naval engineers in Karachi, Pakistan.

June: Terrorists attack the U.S. Consulate in Karachi, Pakistan.

October: Terrorists blow up a popular nightclub in Bali, Indonesia, killing 212. Chechen terrorists occupy a Moscow theater, taking hundreds hostage.

November: Terrorists attempt to take down an Israeli commercial plane over Kenya with shoulder-fired missiles.

Related Organizations

American Civil Liberties Union (ACLU)

125 Broad St., 18th Floor

New York, NY 10004-2400

phone: (212) 549-2500

e-mail: aclu@aclu.org

Web site: www.aclu.org

The American Civil Liberties Union is a national organization that works to defend Americans' civil rights. The ACLU argues that measures to protect national security in the wake of terrorist attacks should not compromise civil liberties. It opposes certain measures in the Patriot Act on these grounds.

Brookings Institution

1775 Massachusetts Ave. NW

Washington, DC 20036

phone: (202) 797-6000

fax: (202) 797-6004

e-mail: brookinfo@brook.edu

Web site: www.brook.edu

The Brookings Institution conducts foreign policy research and analyzes global events, such as terrorist attacks, and their impact on the United States. The institution publishes numerous papers and books on foreign policy and terrorism including "Nasty, Brutish and Long: America's War on Terrorism" and "Protecting the American Homeland: One Year On."

Center for Strategic and International Studies (CSIS)

1800 K St. NW

Washington, DC 20006

phone: (202) 887-0200

fax: (202) 775-3199

Web site: www.csis.org

CSIS is a public policy research institution that focuses on America's economic policy, national security, and foreign and domestic policy. The center analyzes global crises and suggests U.S. military policies, including those which deal with fighting terrorism.

Council on American-Muslim Relations (CAIR)

453 New Jersey Ave. SE

Washington, DC 20003

phone: (202) 488-8787

fax: (202) 488-0833

e-mail: cair@cair-net.org

Web site: www.cair-net.org

CAIR is a nonprofit organization that works to defend the rights of American Muslims. It offers an Islamic perspective on public policy issues. The CAIR Web site features statements condemning the September 11, 2001, terrorist attacks and documents subsequent discrimination against Muslims.

Department of Homeland Security (DHS)

Washington, DC 20528

Web site: www.dhs.gov

The Department of Homeland Security was created after September 11, 2001, and was the largest reshaping of the federal government since 1949. The department is charged with preventing terrorist attacks on American soil, reducing the country's vulnerability to terrorism, and effectively responding to attacks.

Global Exchange

2017 Mission, #303

San Francisco, CA 94110

phone: (415) 255-7296

fax: (415) 255-7498

Web site: www.globalexchange.org

Global Exchange is a human rights organization that seeks to solve global injustice through education, activism, and a noninterventionist U.S. foreign policy. Global Exchange opposes military retaliation to terrorist attacks.

International Policy Institute for Counter-Terrorism (ICT)

PO Box 167

Herzlia, 46150, Israel

phone: 972-9-9527277

fax: 972-9-9513073

e-mail: info@ict.org.il

Web site: www.ict.org.il

This research institute develops public policy solutions to international terrorism. Its Web site is a comprehensive resource on terrorism and counterterrorism, including an extensive database on terrorist organizations.

Islamic Supreme Council of America (ISCA)

1400 Sixteenth St. NW, Room B112

Washington, DC 20036

phone: (202) 939-3400

fax: (202) 939-3410

e-mail: staff@islamicsupremecouncil.org

Web site: www.islamicsupremecouncil.org

The ISCA is a nongovernmental religious organization that promotes Islam in America both by providing practical solutions to American Muslims in integrating Islamic teachings with American culture and by teaching non-Muslims that Islam is a religion of moderation, peace, and tolerance. It strongly condemns Islamic extremists and all forms of terrorism.

Middle East Media Research Institute (MEMRI)

PO Box 27837

Washington, DC 20038-7837

phone: (202) 955-9070

fax: (202) 955-9077

e-mail: memri@memri.org

Web site: www.memri.org

MEMRI translates and disseminates articles and commentaries from Middle East media sources and provides analysis on the political, ideological, intellectual, social, cultural, and religious trends in the region.

Middle East Policy Council (MEPC)

1730 M St. NW, Suite 512

Washington, DC 20036

phone: (202) 296-6767

fax: (202) 296-5791

e-mail: info@mepc.org

Web site: www.mepc.org

This nonprofit organization works on understanding current issues in U.S. relations with countries of the Middle East, including finding solutions to the terrorist problem.

Middle East Research and Information Project (MERIP)

1500 Massachusetts Ave. NW, Suite 119

Washington, DC 20005

phone: (202) 223-3677

fax: (202) 223-3604

e-mail: ctoensing@merip.org

Web site: www.merip.org

MERIP is a nonprofit organization that believes that stereotypes and misconceptions have kept the United States and Europe from fully understanding the Middle East. MERIP aims to end this misunderstanding by addressing a wide range of political, cultural, and social issues and by publishing writings by authors from the Middle East.

National Counterterrorism Center

Web site: www.nctc.gov

The National Counterterrorism Center is charged with informing, empowering, and helping shape the national and international counterterrorism effort to diminish the ranks, capabilities, and activities of current and future terrorists.

Palestinian Media Watch (PMW)

e-mail: webcontact@pmw.org.il

Web site: www.pmw.org.il

PMW monitors Palestinian Arabic language media and schoolbooks for violent and anti-Semitic propaganda. PMW documents articles, lectures, speeches, schoolbooks, cartoons, videos, music, poetry, and other sources that glorify suicide terrorism or otherwise advocate violence.

Terrorism Research Center

phone: (877) 635-0816

Web site: www.terrorism.com

The goal of the Terrorism Research Center is to inform the public on terrorism and information warfare. The site features profiles of terrorist organizations, essays and analysis, and links to other terrorism-related documents and resources.

U.S. Department of State Counterterrorism Office

Office of the Coordinator for Counterterrorism

Office of Public Affairs, Room 2509

U.S. Department of State, 2201 C St. NW

Washington, DC 20520

phone: (202) 647-4000

e-mail via Web site: http://contact-us.state.gov

This federal agency advises the president on foreign policy matters relating to terrorism. The Office of Counterterrorism publishes the annual report *Patterns of Global Terrorism*, a list of the United States' most wanted terrorists, and numerous fact sheets and press releases on the war on terrorism.

Washington Institute for Near East Policy (WINEP)

1828 L St. NW, Suite 1050

Washington, DC 20036

phone: (202) 452-0650

fax: (202) 223-5364

e-mail: info@washingtoninstitute.org

Web site: www.washingtoninstitute.org

WINEP researches and analyzes Middle Eastern issues and U.S. policy in the region. Its Web site features several publications on terrorism.

For Further Research

Books

Graham Allison, *Nuclear Terrorism: The Ultimate Preventable Catastrophe.* New York: Henry Holt, 2004.

Richard A. Clarke, *Against All Enemies: Inside America's War on Terror.* New York: Free Press, 2004.

Clark Kent Ervin, *Open Target: Where America Is Vulnerable to Attack.* New York: Palgrave MacMillan, 2006.

Judith Palmer Harik, *Hezbollah: The Changing Face of Terrorism.* New York: I.B. Tauris, 2004.

Michael Ignatieff, *The Lesser Evil: Political Ethics in an Age of Terror.* Princeton, NJ: Princeton University Press, 2004.

Raphael Israeli, *Islamikaze: Manifestations of Islamic Martyrology.* London: Frank Cass, 2003.

Elaine Landau, *Suicide Bombers: Foot Soldiers of the Terrorist Movement.* New York: Lerner/Twenty-First Century, 2006.

Mahmood Mamdani, *Good Muslim, Bad Muslim: America, the Cold War, and the Roots of Terror.* New York: Pantheon, 2004.

Robert A. Pape, *Dying to Win: The Strategic Logic of Suicide Terrorism.* New York: Random House, 2005.

Christoph Reuter, *My Life Is a Weapon: A Modern History of Suicide Bombing.* Princeton, NJ: Princeton University Press, 2004.

Mark Sageman, *Understanding Terror Networks.* Philadelphia: University of Pennsylvania Press, 2004.

Rosemarie Skaine, *Female Suicide Bombers.* Jefferson, NC: McFarland & Company, 2006.

Periodicals

Neil Altman, "On the Psychology of Suicide Bombing," *Tikkun,* March/April 2005.

William M. Arkin, "The Continuing Misuses of Fear," *Bulletin of the Atomic Scientists,* vol. 62, no. 5, September/October 2006.

Boston Globe, "How Safe a World?" September 11, 2006.

Dorothy Boulware, "Is the USA Ready for War at Home?" *Afro-American,* vol. 114, no. 50, July 29–August 4, 2006.

Lawrence Cunningham, "Don't Call Them Martyrs," *U.S. Catholic,* January 2004.

Stan Crock, "What Makes Suicide Bombers Tick?" *Business Week,* July 6, 2005.

Economist, "The Rational Response to Terrorism," July 23, 2005.

Fred Edwards, "The Issue at Hand," *Humanist,* vol. 66, no. 4, July/August 2006.

Aleya El Bindari-Hammad, "Defusing the Humiliation Bomb," *For a Change,* October/November 2005.

James Fallows, "Declaring Victory," *Atlantic Monthly,* September 2006.

Foreign Policy, "The Terrorism Index," no. 55, July/August 2006.

John Freeman, "Creating a 'Terrorist,'" *Current,* vol. 6, no. 25, June 21–27, 2006.

Norman Friedman, "The Case for Pre-Emption," United States Naval Institute, Proceedings, vol. 132, no. 8, August 2006.

Aparisim Ghosh, "Inside the Mind of an Iraqi Suicide Bomber," *Time,* July 4, 2005.

Bart Kosko, "The Terror Threat May Be Mostly a Bluff," *Los Angeles Times,* September 13, 2004.

Joshua Kurlansink, "Safe or Not? It Depends Who You Ask," *New York Times,* January 28, 2007.

Steven Lasky, "Safe Is a State of Mind," *Security Technology & Design,* vol. 16, no. 10, October 2006.

Scott McConnell, "It's the Occupation, Not the Fundamentalism," *American Conservative,* July 18, 2005.

Henry Morgenstern, "Suicide Terror: Is Law Enforcement Ready?" *Law Enforcement Technology,* September 2006.

John Mueller, "A False Sense of Insecurity?" *Regulation,* Fall 2004.

———, "Is There Still a Terrorist Threat?" *Foreign Affairs,* September/October 2006.

Joseph C. Phillips, "Safe and Secure," *Afro-American Red Star,* vol. 115, no. 3, September 2–8, 2006.

Richard A. Posner, "We Need Our Own MI5," *Washington Post,* August 15, 2006.

Jeffrey Robinson, "Brown's War Just Doesn't Add Up: You Can't Kill Terrorists with a Calculator," *Times Online,* February 14, 2006.

Donald Rumsfeld, "A Force for Good," *Wall Street Journal,* September 11, 2006.

Ziauddin Sardar, "If Suicide Killing Was a Viable Weapon of Just War, Then the Prophet Muhammad Would Have Used It," *New Statesman (1996),* November 28, 2005.

Salil Tripathi, "Debunking the Poverty-Terrorism Myth," *Asian Wall Street Journal,* February 23, 2005.

Internet Sources

Gary S. Becker and Yona Rubinstein, "Fear and the Response to Terrorism: An Economic Analysis," Cornell University ILR School, August 1, 2004. www.ilr.cornell.edu/international/events/upload/BeckerrubinsteinPaper.pdf.

Christopher M. Blanchard, "Al Qaeda: Statements and Evolving Strategy," *CRS Report for Congress, US News & World Report,* June 20, 2005. http://images.usnews.com/usnews/news/articles/050622/alqaeda_crs.pdf.

George W. Bush, "President Bush Discusses Progress in the Global War on Terror," Atlanta GA, White House, September 7, 2006. www.whitehouse.gov/news/releases/2006/09/20060907-2.html.

Leonard A. Cole, "Bioweapons, Proliferation, and the U.S. Anthrax Attack," Center for Contemporary Conflict, 2006. www.ccc.nps.navy.mil//events/recent/Presentations/Cole%20Bio%20paper.pdf.

Federation of American Scientists, "Text of Al-Zarqawi Message Threatening More Attacks," April 6, 2004. www.fas.org/irp/world/para/zarqawi040604.html.

Jomo Gbomo, interview by Brian E. Ross, "ABC News Exclusive: Online Interview with a Terrorist," *ABC News,* January 8, 2007. http://abcnews.go.com/WNT/BrianRoss/story?id=2778701&page=1.

Milton Leitenberg, "Assessing the Biological Weapons and Bioterrorism Threat," Strategic Studies Institute, December 2005. www.terrorisminfo.mipt.org/pdf/Assessing-Biological-Weapons-Bioterrorism-Threat.pdf.

Allison Macfarlane, "All Weapons of Mass Destruction Are Not Equal," *AlterNet,* February 8, 2006. www.alternet.org/story/31510.

Itamar Marcus and Barbara Cook, "Seducing Children to Martyrdom," Teachkidspeace.com, July 4, 2006. www.teachkidspeace.org/doc1027.php.

U.S. Department of Defense, "Press Conference with Secretary of Defense Donald Rumsfeld at the NATO Informal Meeting of Defense Ministers at the St. Bernardin Hotel, Portoroz, Slovenia," September 28, 2006. www.defenselink.mil/Transcripts/Transcript.aspx?TranscriptID=3737.

U.S. State Department, *Country Reports on Terrorism,* 2005. www.state.gov/s/ct/rls/crt/c17689.htm.

White House, "Interview of the Vice President by Tim Russert, NBC News, Meet the Press," September 10, 2006. www.whitehouse.gov/news/releases/2006/09/20060910.html.

Heather Wokusch, "Who's the Real WMD Threat? How the Bush Administration's Biological Weapons Buildup Affects You," *Antiwar.com,* April 15, 2005. www.antiwar.com/orig/wokusch.php?articleid=5564.

Source Notes

Overview

1. Robert A. Pape, *Dying to Win: The Strategic Logic of Suicide Terrorism.* New York: Random House, 2005, p. 2.
2. Abraham D. Sofaer, testimony before the National Commission on Terrorist Attacks Upon the United States, March 31, 2003. www.9-11commission.gov.
3. Chris Short, "NYCLU Loses in NYC Subway Bag Search Case," *Jawa Report,* December 2, 2005.
4. Steve Filyo and Leo West, "The Suicide Bomber," *Retail Traffic,* September 1, 2005.
5. James D. Zirin, "Fearful Patriot Act?" *Washington Times,* October 22, 2004, p. A18.
6. Richard A. Posner, "We Need Our Own MI5," *Washington Post,* August 15, 2006, p. A13.
7. Russell Feingold, address to the U.S. Senate, Washington, DC, October 25, 2001. http://feingold.senate.gov.
8. Nicole Colson, "Big Brother Is Watching You," *Socialist Worker,* January 27, 2006, pp. 8–9.
9. Fred Edwards, "The Issue at Hand," *Humanist,* vol. 66, no. 4, July/August 2006, p. 3.
10. Steve Coll, "Citizens (Talk of the Town)," *New Yorker,* June 5, 2006, p. 27.
11. House of Commons, *Report of the Official Account of the Bombings in London on 7th July 2005.* London: Stationary Office, May 11, 2006, p. 26.
12. Anna Quindlen, "A Nation's Fear of Flying," *Newsweek,* August 21, 2006, p. 100.
13. Ted Lewis and Jason Mark, "Terrorism Is Not Inevitable," *AlterNet,* June 12, 2002. www.alternet.org.
14. *Boston Globe,* "How Safe a World?" September 11, 2006.
15. Quoted in Stephan Faris, "Containment Strategy," *Atlantic Monthly,* December 2006, p. 34.
16. Quoted in Faris, "Containment Strategy," p. 34.

How Serious Is the Problem of Terrorism?

17. U.S. Department of State, *Country Reports on Terrorism,* 2005. www.state.gov.
18. Gary S. Becker and Yona Rubinstein, "Fear and the Response to Terrorism: An Economic Analysis," School of Industrial and Labor Relations, Cornell University, August 1, 2004, p. 46. www.ilr.cornell.edu.
19. James F. Jarboe, "The Threat of Eco-Terrorism," testimony before the House Resources Committee, Subcommittee on Forests and Forest Health, February 12, 2002. www.fbi.gov.
20. *Economist,* "The Rational Response to Terrorism," July 23, 2005, p. 72.
21. Leonard A. Cole, "Bioweapons, Proliferation, and the U.S. Anthrax Attack," Center for Contemporary Conflict, 2006. www.ccc.nps.navy.mil.
22. George Tenet, "Written Statement for the Record of the Director of Central Intelligence Before the National Commission on Terrorist Attacks Upon the United States," March 24, 2004, p. 32. www.cia.gov.
23. Richard Ebright, "Letter," *Science,* vol. 307, no. 5714, March 4, 2005, pp. 1,409–1,410.
24. Allison Macfarlane, "All Weapons of Mass Destruction Are Not Equal,"

AlterNet, February 8, 2006. www.alter net.org.
25. Noah Shachtman, "Bigger Worries than BioChem," *TCS Daily,* October 8, 2003.
26. William M. Arkin, "The Continuing Misuses of Fear," *Bulletin of the Atomic Scientists,* vol. 62, no. 5, September/ October 2006, pp. 42–45.
27. John Mueller, "A False Sense of Insecurity?" *Regulation,* Fall 2004.
28. Bart Kosko, "The Terror Threat May Be Mostly a Bluff," *Los Angeles Times,* September 13, 2004, p. B11.

Why Do People Commit Terrorist Acts?

29. *Economist,* "Shireen and Others Like Her," May 22, 2004.
30. Pape, *Dying to Win,* p. 2.
31. Osama bin Laden, "Text of Fatwah Urging Jihad Against Americans," *al-Quds al-'Arabi,* February 23, 1998.
32. Robert A. Pape, interview by Scott McConnell, "It's the Occupation, Not the Fundamentalism," *American Conservative,* July 18, 2005.
33. Abu Musab al-Zarqawi, "'Text' of Al-Zarqawi Message Threatening More Attacks," Federation of American Scientists, April 6, 2004. www.fas.org.
34. *Boston Globe,* "How Safe a World?"
35. *Boston Globe,* "How Safe a World?"
36. Pape, *Dying to Win,* p. 36.
37. Raphael Israeli, *Islamikaze: Manifestations of Islamic Martyrology.* London: Frank Cass, 2003, p. 48.
38. Quoted in Aparisim Ghosh, "Inside the Mind of an Iraqi Suicide Bomber," *Time,* July 4, 2005, p. 22.
39. Quoted in Aparisim Ghosh, "Professor of Death," *Time,* October 24, 2005, p. 44.
40. Ziauddin Sardar, "If Suicide Killing Was a Viable Weapon of Just War, Then the Prophet Muhammad Would Have Used It," *New Statesman,* November 28, 2005, p. 26.
41. Neil Altman, "On the Psychology of Suicide Bombing," *Tikkun,* March/ April 2005, p. 15.
42. Jomo Gbomo, interview by Brian E. Ross, "ABC News Exclusive: Online Interview with a Terrorist," *ABC News,* January 8, 2007. http://abcnews.go.com.
43. Aleya El Bindari-Hammad, "Defusing the Humiliation Bomb," *For a Change,* October/November 2005, p. 24.
44. Israeli, *Islamikaze,* p. 48.
45. Diane Feinstein, "Global Poverty and the War on Terrorism," speech before the Los Angeles World Affairs Council, March 28, 2002. www.lawac.org.
46. Salil Tripathi, "Debunking the Poverty-Terrorism Myth," *Asian Wall Street Journal,* February 23, 2005.
47. Alan B. Krueger, "Poverty Doesn't Create Terrorists," *New York Times,* May 29, 2003.
48. El Bindari-Hammad, "Defusing the Humiliation Bomb," p. 24.

How Are Terrorist Attacks Carried Out?

49. *Economist,* "Martyrdom and Murder—Suicide Terrorism," January 10, 2004.
50. Quoted in *Foreign Policy,* "The Terrorism Index," no. 155, July/August 2006, pp. 48–56.
51. Pape, interview by McConnell.
52. Quoted in Itamar Marcus and Barbara Cook, "Seducing Children to Martyrdom," Teachkidspeace.com, July 4, 2006.
53. Quoted in Middle East Media Research Institute, "Egyptian Weekly on Hezbollah's Armed Children's Militias," Special Dispatch Series no. 1276, September 1, 2006.
54. David Brooks, "The Culture of Martyrdom," *Atlantic Monthly,* June 2002.
55. Quoted in Simon Elegant, "On Terror's Trail," *Time International,* October 17, 2005.

56. Quoted in Ghosh, "Inside the Mind of an Iraqi Suicide Bomber."
57. Quoted in Ghosh, "Professor of Death."
58. Quoted in Ghosh, "Professor of Death."
59. Quoted in Ghosh, "Professor of Death."
60. Mohammed Mumtaz Tanweer, quoted in Shiv Malik, "The Suicide Bomber in His Own Words," *New Statesman (1996),* July 3, 2006, p. 26.

How Can Terrorist Attacks Be Prevented?

61. Joseph C. Phillips, "Safe and Secure," *Afro-American Red Star,* vol. 115, no. 3, September 2–8, 2006, p. A13.
62. *Houston Chronicle,* "Fluid Solution," August 11, 2006, p. 8.
63. Stephen E. Flynn and James M. Loy, "A Port in the Storm over Dubai," *New York Times,* February 28, 2006.
64. George W. Bush, "President Bush Discusses Progress in the Global War on Terror," Atlanta, Georgia, White House, September 7, 2006. www.whitehouse.gov.
65. Steven Lasky, "Safe Is a State of Mind," *Security Technology & Design,* vol. 16, no. 10, October 2006, p. 8.
66. Dick Cheney, "Interview of the Vice President by Tim Russert, NBC News, Meet the Press," White House, September 10, 2006. www.whitehouse.gov.
67. Donald Rumsfeld, "Press Conference with Secretary of Defense Donald Rumsfeld at the NATO Informal Meeting of Defense Ministers at the St. Bernardin Hotel, Portoroz, Slovenia," U.S. Department of Defense, September 28, 2006. www.defenselink.mil.
68. Quoted in *CBSnews.com,* "Rumsfeld Skeptical of Intel Analysis: Secretary Says It's Impossible to Know Whether Wars Created More Terror," September 26, 2006.
69. Edward M. Kennedy, "New National Intelligence Estimate Determines That the Misguided War Has 'Metastasized and Spread' Terrorism," statement, September 23, 2006. http://kennedy.senate.gov.
70. Maurice R. Greenberg, "Terrorist Financing: Report of an Independent Task Force," Council on Foreign Relations, 2002.
71. George W. Bush, "'President Freezes Terrorists' Assets,' Remarks by the President, Secretary of the Treasury O'Neill and Secretary of State Powell on Executive Order," Rose Garden, White House, September 24, 2001. www.whitehouse.gov.
72. Greenberg, "Terrorist Financing."
73. *Economist,* "Looking for Terrorism in All the Wrong Places," October 14, 2005.
74. *Economist,* "Bali, Again; Indonesia," October 8, 2005.
75. Jeffrey Robinson, "Brown's War Just Doesn't Add Up: You Can't Kill Terrorists with a Calculator," *Times Online,* February 14, 2006.
76. *New York Times,* "In Tapes, Receipts and a Diary, Details of the British Terror Case. (Foreign Desk)," August 28, 2006.
77. Posner, "We Need Our Own MI5," p. A13.
78. James Fallows, "Declaring Victory," *Atlantic Monthly,* September 2006, pp. 60–73.
79. *Detroit News,* "9/11: Five Years Later, Are We Safe Enough?" September 11, 2006, p. A6.

List of Illustrations

How Serious Is the Problem of Terrorism?

Why Do People Commit Terrorist Attacks?

How Are Terrorist Attacks Carried Out?

How Can Terrorist Attacks Be Prevented?

Index

About the Author

Lauri S. Friedman earned her bachelor's degree in religion and political science from Vassar College. Her studies there focused on political Islam, and she produced a thesis on the Islamic Revolution in Iran titled *Neither West, Nor East, but Islam.* She also holds a preparatory degree in flute performance from the Manhattan School of Music.

Her other publications for ReferencePoint Press include *Compact Research: The Death Penalty.* She has also edited numerous publications for Greenhaven Press on controversial social issues such as gay marriage, Islam, terrorism, racism, assisted suicide, and the Patriot Act.

Friedman lives near the beach in San Diego with her partner, Randy, and their yellow lab, Trucker.